Shaw turned h... his computer, leaving Eviana to stare first at him, then down at her notebook.

The worst thing about this man was that he moved through life all power and control. And then out of the blue, he gifted her with words that touched on her deepest fears, soothed them, made her feel as though she could truly do this. Not just help the Harrington Foundation reestablish itself, but become a leader, someone her people could depend upon. Shaw Harrington was a dangerous man. The more she got to know him, the more she felt herself slipping down a dangerous slope.

One she suspected that, if she fell too far, would result in her leaving broken pieces of her heart in Edinburgh.

Dear Reader,

When I started research for *Royally Forbidden to the Boss*, I typed *castles* into Pinterest and saw beautiful castles from around the world, including Neuschwanstein Castle in Germany and Bojnice Castle in Slovakia. But it was Edinburgh Castle that caught my attention, standing tall and proud yet isolated on a massive rock, overlooking the city. Not only is it a stunning structure, but it reminded me of my hero and heroine, Eviana and Shaw. These two hold themselves to incredibly high standards and keep their hearts guarded against failure...and love. Writing Eviana and Shaw trying to resist their growing attraction as they work together to save Shaw's charitable foundation was so much fun, as was incorporating real places from Scotland and England. I hope you enjoy watching them embrace who they truly are as they fall in love. Happy reading!

Scarlett

ROYALLY FORBIDDEN TO THE BOSS

SCARLETT CLARKE

ROMANCE

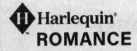

Harlequin®
ROMANCE

ISBN-13: 978-1-335-21624-3

Recycling programs for this product may not exist in your area.

Royally Forbidden to the Boss

Harlequin Enterprises ULC
22 Adelaide St. West, 41st Floor
Toronto, Ontario M5H 4E3, Canada
www.Harlequin.com

Printed in U.S.A.

Scarlett Clarke's interest in romance can be traced back to her love of Nancy Drew books, when she tried to solve the mysteries of her favorite detective while rereading the romantic chapters with Ned Nickerson. She's thrilled to now be writing romances of her own. Scarlett lives in, and loves, her hometown of Kansas City. By day she works in public relations and wrangles two toddlers, two cats and a dog. By night she writes romance and tries to steal a few moments with her firefighter hubby.

Also by Scarlett Clarke

The Prince She Kissed in Paris

To my mom and husband.
It was a mad dash to the finish line,
but you made it possible.

CHAPTER ONE

Eviana

Princess Eviana Adamovic had less than a second to register the wave coming at her before it hit. She sucked in a shuddering gasp as chilly rainwater splashed her face and soaked the left side of her body. Brakes screeched as she bit back a curse.

You have got *to be kidding me.*

Her neighbors waking her up at five o'clock with a very loud argument over someone's flirty coworker had been the first sign that today wasn't going to go according to plan. Her early wake-up had been followed by her coffee machine sending a cascade of much-needed caffeine down the front of her cabinet after she'd overfilled it.

And now… Eviana looked down and sighed. She'd picked one of her best suits for today, a couture black blazer and pants with Louboutin pumps. It was now soaked through. A splash of mud on her white blouse added an extra flair to her debacle of a morning.

A car door slammed.

"Are you all right?"

The voice wrapped around her, deep and masculine. She raised her head. And froze.

The man standing in front of her was both unbelievably handsome and incredibly intimidating. Dark red hair combed back from a broad forehead. Strong slashes of cheekbone above a beard cut to precision along an angular jaw. A three-piece suit expertly tailored to follow the broadness of his shoulders and accommodate his impressive height. He stood nearly a foot taller than her.

Deep blue eyes fixed on hers. Something flared, a look of surprise, perhaps, before a shutter dropped over them.

"Yes." A brisk wind swept down the road and pierced her now sodden coat. "Just…chilly." She glanced down at her shirt again and grimaced. "And dirty."

"I apologize. I didn't realize how deep the puddle was."

Scottish, judging by rolling *r*s and melodic cadence of his words. But there was a blunt roughness in his voice that, coupled with the hardness in his face, told her he was in just about as good of a mood as she was.

"It's…fine." It wasn't, but the man had stopped when most would have just kept driving.

"How much do I owe you for the suit?"

"It'll wash out." She patted the maroon-colored

leather bag she'd thankfully had on her right side. "And I have a change of clothes, too."

"Can I drive you somewhere?"

Her head shot up in surprise. "Excuse me?"

He gestured to the empty street. "Few taxis at this hour. The bus won't be by for another twenty minutes."

"You're not trying to kidnap me, are you?" she said, only half joking.

He stared at her for a moment. Then one corner of his mouth slowly curved up.

Vau. A different kind of shiver traced its way down her spine. If the man could stir that kind of reaction with just the hint of a smile, what would a real one do?

"No, I'm not trying to kidnap you."

Don't even think about it.

But she was. It wasn't just the man's good looks, although that certainly didn't hurt. No, there was something…compelling about him. That bare-bones smile, a distinct contrast to the tension that rolled off his muscular frame, the faint darkness in his eyes.

Cold reality smothered temptation. That and one of the palace's many rules filtering through her mind:

Princesses do not ride alone in cars with men unless they are related by blood or serving in a security role.

"I appreciate you stopping. And offering a ride.

But I'm only a block away from my office. And," she added with a smile to take any potential sting out of her words, "I would probably give my brother a heart attack if I accepted a ride from a stranger."

Again that twitch of the lips that made her stomach do a long, slow roll. "Your brother sounds like a smart man."

"He is."

Although if Nicholai knew everything she was up to, from the tiny apartment she'd rented to walking to work with only a private bodyguard following nearly a block behind, he wouldn't have a heart attack. He'd fly to Scotland and drag her back to Kelna without a second thought.

Her mystery man pulled out a black leather wallet. "At least let me give you money for dry cleaning."

The man was clearly wealthy, from his bespoke suit to the gleaming black Rolls-Royce parked just behind him. But she couldn't do it. Not when she had a walk-in closet full of clothes back at the palace, dresses and skirts and blouses from designers around the world.

"I really do think the mud will come out."

He held out a banknote, the value of which made her eyebrows shoot up.

"Take it."

Her eyes narrowed at the insistence in his tone. She'd been spoiled the last two months, living her life on her own terms. Having someone tell her what to do to rankled.

"How about you offer me a tenth of that for coffee and a pastry?"

"Are you always this stubborn?"

"Yes." She cocked her head to one side. "Are you?"

His fingers tightened on the banknote. Then, slowly, he tucked it back into his wallet.

"Yes."

The resignation in his tone tugged at her.

"Here."

He held out a much more reasonable amount, although still double what she had suggested. Eviana started to reach for it, then stopped as an idea flared. It was a ridiculous idea. But as she stared at her handsome stranger, longing wound its way through her veins.

Could he hear her heart pounding as the idea sank its roots deeper? See the pulse pounding in her throat? She'd invited plenty of men to join her for coffee before—parliamentarians, ambassadors, visiting dignitaries, wealthy businessmen.

But they'd all known who she was. Never had she invited a man for personal reasons for…well, anything.

A princess is never bold.

Except she wasn't a princess. Not right now. She was just Ana Barros, intern for a boutique public relations firm in Edinburgh. Princess Eviana wouldn't have been able to invite a random stranger to coffee.

But Ana could.

Her heart galloped in her chest. "I'll accept it on one condition."

One eyebrow arched up. "Oh?"

"You let me buy you coffee."

His lips parted as a V appeared between his brows. "What?"

She nodded her head toward the row of buildings that lined the street with what she hoped was a casual gesture. The windows of one glowed with yellow light, beckoning early morning commuters and random passersby to stop.

"Braw Roasterie. They make the best cortados."

"I stick to black coffee."

"They make that, too."

"Why?"

She bit back a grin. Beneath his grumpy tone, she sensed that Mr. Rolls-Royce was flustered.

"You look like you could use it. That and five minutes of sitting with nothing to do."

His lips parted slightly before he looked over his shoulder at the coffee shop. For one moment, she thought he was actually going to say yes.

Then he glanced down at his watch. "I should get going."

Disappointment lanced through her. He struck her as the kind of man who kept a rigorous schedule, one that didn't allow for situations like splashing chilly puddle water on a pedestrian. She wanted to push, to encourage him to break free for just a few minutes.

But she wasn't going to be that person, wasn't going to push. She knew all too well how it felt to be pushed. Besieged. Cornered.

"All right. Thanks again for stopping."

She started walking.

"Wait." She turned back just in time to see him hold up the money. "You forgot something."

A princess exhibits gratitude and grace at all times.

She grinned at him. "I said I'd only accept it on one condition. So no, I didn't."

The surprise on his face almost made getting drenched worth it. She gave him a friendly wave and kept walking.

Helena, the head of the palace's public relations department, would have had steam coming out of her ears if she'd witnessed Eviana decline a gift. A thought that added an extra bounce to Eviana's step as she moved down the sidewalk.

It felt good, so good, to just…be. To talk with a stranger without monitoring every word that passed her lips. To tease, invite, converse without wondering if Helena or one of the public relations minions was going to show up outside her door later and provide her with a detailed list of what she'd done wrong. Even if the man behind her had refused her invitation, just the fact that she had been able to invite someone to coffee without worrying about photos being taken and splashed across social media was a win.

Not to mention, she thought with a small smile, getting to talk with a very handsome man for a few minutes. No expectations, no pretenses.

She almost glanced over her shoulder. One last look.

And then decided not to. She could have done without mud and rainwater. But her interaction with the Scottish stranger had been a pleasant anomaly in the midst of a chaotic morning. One that had made her feel both normal and more like…like a woman, she decided with a satisfied smile. Something made all the more precious with the few weeks she had left before returning to her former life.

Perhaps, she thought as she opened the door to Braw Roasterie and inhaled the rich scent of roasted coffee beans, her morning had turned out just right.

CHAPTER TWO

Shaw

WARMTH SPILLED OUT from the open doorway. A group of men and women in suits poured out of Braw Roasterie onto the street, talking and laughing even as they all checked their watches.

Shaw stood back, eyes trained on the woman sitting in the corner of the shop, her attention focused on a notebook as her pen darted across the page. She must have changed while he'd parked his car and walked back. Instead of the black pants and white shirt he'd glimpsed beneath her raincoat, she now wore a bright yellow skirt and an ivory blouse dotted with blue flowers. He'd talked with the woman for less than five minutes, but the outfit she had on now seemed more…her. Vibrant, colorful. The cascade of blond hair falling down her back seemed more natural, too, versus the tightly wound bun that had been at the nape of her neck.

Although a downside of her hair hanging loose was that it partially obscured her face—a stunningly unique face that had made him look twice when he'd gotten out to check on the pedestrian he had unintentionally drenched on his early morning drive. *Ethereal* was the first word that had come to mind. Wide-set green eyes, a bow-shaped mouth, romantic features offset by a pointed chin that hinted at defiance. Her easygoing acceptance of the whole incident and declining of the money had struck him, too.

Not just struck him, he admitted as the crowd cleared and he moved toward the door. Intrigued him. Enough that he'd pulled into a parking space and sat, deliberating on his next action for a solid five minutes before he'd succumbed to his curiosity and walked back to the coffee shop.

He didn't do things like this—spontaneous meetings with random people he met on the street. He barely came out of his office at all.

What am I doing?

He didn't have an answer. Only that driving away from the woman who had rejected his money and bounced off with a smile and a cheeky wave had seemed like the worst possible thing he could do.

Numerous scents hit him at once as he walked into Braw Roasterie. The earthy boldness of coffee underlined with chocolatey sweetness. Freshly baked bread and rich butter. Soft music played from hidden speakers. Gleaming wood tables played hosts to wrought-iron chairs. A well-maintained shop, one that he had passed by for years.

He squared his shoulders and moved toward the blonde woman's table. His dating life had been stagnant the past few months. But just last year he'd dated a corporate lawyer for nearly five months and a software engineer for a Fortune 500 company the year prior to that. Women who had been interesting enough yet just as focused as he was on their careers, on things other than what most people wanted out of relationships: love, marriage, family. Those things he had zero interest in. He didn't want, or need, anyone in his life. Not when getting the Harrington Foundation back on track required his full attention. Not when the last person he had trusted had taken his trust and ripped it to tatters, along with the reputation of the organization he'd dedicated his life to creating.

Yet in the span of a few minutes, this woman had crawled under his skin. She might have been pretending that she didn't know who he was, but he'd bet half his fortune her lack of recognition had been genuine. Her casual grace, coupled with that impish defiance, had been a breath of fresh air. He normally surrounded himself with competent, emotionally removed individuals. A strategy that had served him well.

Perhaps too well, he mused as he sidestepped a sleepy-looking couple pushing a stroller. He'd kept people at a distance for so long that one encounter outside of his normal routine had upset his balance. Had made him think there was something special about this woman to the point that he had backtracked and was now seventeen minutes behind schedule.

Just five more minutes. Five minutes to talk to the woman, prove there was nothing unique aside from an unusual encounter early in the morning, and move on with his life.

A light, floral scent floated beneath the homey smells as he drew near. His shadow fell across her table. She looked up…

And smiled at him. Not the teasing grin or sassy smirk she'd given him earlier but a true smile, one that made her eyes crinkle at the corners. As if she were genuinely happy to see him.

His world shifted.

"Hello."

Her voice, regal and composed yet warm and layered with that musical accent he couldn't place, pulled at him. Made him long for something he hadn't even realized he'd wanted.

"I decided to take you up on your offer."

She stood, the brightness of her smile matching the eye-popping yellow of her skirt. "I'm glad. Cortado and a black coffee?"

"Just the coffee."

"How about I order you both and if you hate

the cortado, then you have the black coffee to fall back on?"

Phrased like that, and accompanied by that smile he couldn't stop staring at, he simply nodded.

Dhia, what was wrong with him?

She moved to the bar and ordered two cortados and a black coffee. Her butchered attempt at Gaelic had him pressing his lips together and looking away as the barista laughingly coached her through the phrases.

He handed her the twenty-pound note he'd offered earlier, which she accepted with a thank-you as she slid it across the bar and told the barista to keep the change.

"Not many people bother to learn Gaelic," he said as they moved off to the side.

"I love the sound of it. It's unlike any other language I've learned. I've only been learning for six weeks. I sound atrocious," she said with a laugh.

"But English is not your native language?"

"No." She hesitated, the barest pause. "Croatian is my first language. I also speak Italian and a little bit of French."

"And how does a girl from Southeastern Europe end up here?"

Another hesitation, along with a slash of pink along her elegant cheekbones.

"Taking a break from home," she finally said.

Her answer surprised him, as did the fatigue in her voice, the quiet sadness on her face.

Like looking in a mirror.

"Stepping away is never easy."

She drew in a deep breath, then slowly released it. When she looked at him, the sparkle was gone, replaced by a maturity that altered his previous impression of a sunny young woman who had known little hardship.

No, this woman was someone far more dangerous. Someone who had experienced hardship and overcome. Someone dynamic and complex and interesting.

Someone he wanted to know.

"No, it's not. But sometimes necessary."

Necessary. Crucial. The only way to survive when the life you knew shattered in the blink of an eye.

For twenty years, Shaw had had no problems keeping everyone at arm's length. When the doctor had come out to tell him his mother hadn't made it—the same doctor who had brushed aside Shaw's concerns the week prior when his mother had gone in for a checkup with a *trust me, she's fine*—a switch had been flipped. He'd mentally drawn a line that separated him from the rest of the world. To this day, he'd never been tempted to cross it. Never been tempted to let feelings past the wall he'd built, stone by stone, in the weeks after his mother's death that separated the boy he'd been and the man fate had fashioned over-night with one cruel blow.

Yet for the first time in two decades, words rose in his throat. A desire to share with another human being. One he had a gut feeling would understand more than anyone he'd met in a long time. The challenge of the past few months. The stress, the frustration, the deep-seated grief at realizing his decision to step away from the foundation had cost so much.

"Two cortados and a black coffee!"

The barista's boisterous announcement broke the spell. Shaw stepped back. A small move, but he saw the confusion in the blonde woman's eyes, followed by the smoothing of her features. Unnerving to watch, although he'd been accused of doing the same thing himself—hiding his thoughts and emotions behind a mask.

"I hope you enjoy your drinks."

He frowned. Still her voice, still soft and flowing. But the cheerful energy had disappeared, replaced by a smooth, practiced cadence that sounded...bland. Colorless.

"Thank you."

Shaw reached for his drinks at the same time she reached for hers. Their hands brushed. The faintest touch, but it shot through him like a bolt of lightning. He forced himself to grab the cups and face her. Judging by the twin splotches of color in her cheeks, she'd felt it, too.

He allowed himself a moment. Just one moment to imagine what he would do if life was different. If life hadn't taught him at a young age that trust was not something to lightly give nor receive. If his former friend and colleague hadn't destroyed years of hard work. If he was capable of offering anyone more than the wealth he'd painstakingly built over the years.

A fantasy. One that would never be. Six months later and he was still staring down the barrel of a crisis that had no end in sight. A crisis he had created by giving a grain of trust to someone he had thought qualified to lead, to do what he couldn't. Even if Zach hadn't dragged the foundation to the edge of annihilation, Shaw had no interest in breaching the wall he'd carefully maintained for so long. A wall that kept him immune to pain and heartbreak.

No one would ever be worth the risk of that kind of pain again.

"Enjoy the rest of your day."

He didn't wait for her response. He stalked outside, hands wrapped around the cups, his steps firm and determined. The farther he got from the shop, the more the band of tension around his chest loosened. It was like coming out of a dream. One where, for a moment, he'd been tempted to ask a woman on a date. Not for an event, not for mutual companionship, but because he'd wanted to get to know her better.

Sun broke through the clouds as Shaw reached his car. He breathed out. The strain of the last few months, as well as poor sleep, had left him vulnerable to emotions he rarely experienced. It was only natural, he told himself, that an odd encounter with an attractive stranger would have sucked him in, made him behave out of character.

As he started the car, he glanced at the two cups he'd placed in the cup holders. Then, slowly, he raised the smaller cup to his lips. Rich espresso and sweet milk hit his tongue, an indulgent blend that made his black coffee seem bitter and boring.

With a frustrated sigh, he set the cortado down and picked up his coffee. His life didn't need change. At least his personal life. He had been content before this morning's events. And as to the professional aspects, the meeting he had scheduled two hours from now would hopefully be a step toward getting the Harrington Foundation back on track.

Content, he told himself as he pulled away from the curb and kept his gaze fixed on the road ahead. *I'm content.*

He ignored the little voice whispering *Liar* as he drove away.

CHAPTER THREE

Eviana

THE OFFICE SPACE for Murray PR was the size of a large walk-in closet. Big enough for Kirstin Murray's L-shaped desk, two tufted leather chairs arranged around a small coffee table and Eviana's own tiny desk shoved up against one of the two windows. The wall behind Kirstin's desk was taken up by a glass dry-erase board, the surface covered with scribbles, notes and schedules. The other wall featured framed photos of Kirstin's clients to date.

Eviana hummed to herself as she flicked on the lights and savored the small flicker of joy she always felt walking into the office. When she'd finally decided to take up her brother on the offer of a sabbatical, he'd suggested somewhere lush and tropical. The Seychelles or Belize.

But she hadn't wanted a mindless vacation. She'd needed a place where she could breathe, yes, but also a place she could explore herself, regain her confidence, maybe even learn something that would help her handle the ever-increasing demands of royal life.

Demands she wasn't sure she could handle.

She moved to the windows, crossing her arms as she gazed out over the country that had been her salvation. When she'd searched for relaxing destinations, there had been the usual results for beaches and mountain resorts tucked away from prying eyes. But seeing pictures of the rolling green hills of Scotland, the white sandy beaches, the winding cobblestone streets…it had called to something in her. Traces of home evident in the history, the old architecture, yet still somewhere completely new.

Kelna would always be her home. But after her time here, Scotland would rank a close second.

She glanced down at the street below and smiled when she glimpsed a familiar figure seated on a bench across the street. The one stipulation her brother, Nicholai, had demanded when she'd asked for a few months off had been a bodyguard. Jodi was not only an incredible bodyguard but seemed to understand Eviana's need for space, for a simple life without the trappings of palace royalty.

A soft sigh filled the quiet of the office.

Poor little princess.

It felt wrong. This discontent, this looming sensation of dread as her July deadline drew near. She'd been granted twelve weeks. The first eight had gone by in the blink of an eye, although she didn't regret a second of how she'd spent them. Having the chance to live independently, to work and apply herself, to not only do things right but make mistakes without the palace watching and critiquing her, was something she had desperately needed.

She glanced back at the planning board. At the words written cockeyed around schedules, names of contacts and random ideas jotted down during meetings. It was utter chaos.

And she loved it.

Everything at the palace was regimented, even more so in the months leading up to and after her father's passing as she'd taken on new duties. There'd been days when she'd been scheduled down to the last minute. No flexibility, no room for error.

At first, it had been a godsend. The frenetic pace had left her tired and tumbling into bed at the end of long days that had sometimes stretched into even longer nights. It had also left her with little time to remember that her father, her *otac*, was dying. Once he'd passed, she'd thrown herself in even deeper, ignoring the warning signs slowly piling up. But as the meetings had increased, as she'd tried to maintain a diplomatic face at the ever-increasing number of public engagements she'd been requested to attend, the stress had pressed in on her. Strained her to the breaking point.

Until she'd broken.

Eviana scrunched her eyes shut, swallowed. One deep breath, then another.

You are more than a crown.

How many times had her soon-to-be sister-in-law Madeline said that to her in the last year or so? Encouraged her to speak her mind, to let her personality shine through? Something that was easy for Madeline to do when she'd been raised to be independent and strong, not an ornament loved by her father but essentially raised by the females on the palace staff. Women who had encouraged Eviana from as far back as she could remember to be proper. Graceful. Regal.

A small smile curved her lips as she imagined Madeline's face if she ever shared the differences in how they'd been raised. Madeline was one of the best things to ever happen to their family. Eviana loved her brother with all her heart. But until he'd met Madeline, he hadn't let anyone help, had hoarded the numerous duties he'd been saddled with as their father's health had steadily declined. It hadn't been until he and Madeline had shared an illicit kiss in the gardens and made international headlines that he had finally confronted his inability to ask for help.

Yet the improvement in her and her brother's relationship had come with a price. Namely her increased involvement in palace affairs.

Eviana turned away from the window and stepped over to her desk. Nicholai hadn't asked—she had volunteered. Kelna was growing rapidly. Between the new seaport and the increased media attention from Nicholai and Madeline's upcoming wedding, their hidden gem of a country had become the focal point of international interest.

That, too, had come with a price. One that demanded so much more of her, of Nicholai, even of Madeline. Their time, their effort.

What if I can't give enough?

The thought whispered through her mind, a cruel taunt that slowly pulled up a memory she'd tried to keep buried deep. It had been nearly three months now. But the hot sting of embarrassment, the nauseous ball of shame in the pit of her stomach as she'd stumbled through a speech in front of dozens of Kelnian business owners, the flood of tears she had barely kept contained until she'd made it back to the receiving room.

There had been no triggers. Nothing concrete she could put her finger on when Helena had followed her into the room and demanded to know what had happened. One minute she had been fine and the next she hadn't.

The coverage had been thankfully minimal, no doubt smoothed over by Helena's minions working in tandem with the media to spin a story about a tired, grieving princess. But it had been enough of an incident that Nicholai had told her to take some time away.

Eviana sank into her chair. When she returned to Kelna, she would not only be returning home but coming back to a list of even more duties and responsibilities she'd never before contemplated. Speaking at galas, military processions and national holidays, something Nicholai or their father had previously done. Serving as the patron of numerous charities, not just her select few that currently revolved around healthcare. Hosting visiting dignitaries, especially when Nicholai was in other meetings or taking some much-needed time off with Madeline. Duties he insisted he still trusted her with, even if she didn't trust herself to do them.

Or you don't want to do.

Her shoulders drooped. Dueling doubts plagued her even as she moved through this fantasy of a temporary life away from the spotlight. Had she failed because she wasn't capable of leading? Or worse, had she faltered because, deep down, she was selfish and didn't want to follow the rules of her own country? Didn't want to do what so many had done before her and pledge her identity to the crown?

If this morning was any indicator, she'd pick the latter. When the handsome stranger had shown up, the leap in her pulse had been far too strong to excuse as simple excitement. No, she'd been interested. Very interested.

Except where could it have gone? A few dates before she disappeared back to her life in Kelna while she pretended to be someone she wasn't? A one-night stand?

Princesses do not have one-night stands.

Imagining that on Helena's lengthy list of rules brought a much-needed smile to Eviana's face. As much as the man's abrupt departure had stung, it had been a reprieve. She never should have invited him to coffee in the first place. The invitation hadn't been rooted in throwing caution to the wind or living life to the fullest.

It had been rooted in desire. Arrogance. A momentary lapse in judgment.

At least I won't have to see him again.

Footsteps sounded outside the door.

Kirstin breezed into the room, silver hair pushed back from her angular face with a red headband.

"Good morning, Ana!"

Whether it was the events of the morning or Eviana's dip into the past that had left her emotionally raw, she couldn't contain her flinch at the use of the name she'd been using ever since she'd landed in Scotland. It was a nickname, one she had faint memories of her mother using. But she was using it, and her mother's maiden name, under false pretenses.

She shoved her misgivings to the side and smiled at the woman who had become not only her boss and mentor but a good friend.

"Good morning." She glanced at the oversized coffee cup in Kirstin's hand. "Rough night?"

"More like I couldn't sleep." Kirstin beamed from ear to ear as she set the coffee cup down and punched a button on her computer screen. "We have a meeting with the Harrington Foundation!"

"That's wonderful!"

Kirstin's smile dimmed a fraction. "You have no idea what I'm talking about, do you?"

"No," Eviana said with another small smile, "but judging by your reaction, it's big."

"It's bigger than big. This is what I've been waiting for. The account that will catapult Murray PR to the top."

Excitement clashed with a faint sense of foreboding. One of the reasons why she had applied for Kirstin's internship was because she worked with smaller organizations, ones primarily based in Scotland. Eviana's risk of exposure was minimal.

God, how self-absorbed can you be? Her friend had just gotten incredible news, and here she was, worried about herself.

"Okay," she said with enthusiasm to cover her lapse, "so fill me in—everything I need to know, and most importantly, where do we start?"

A knock sounded on the door.

"Oh, goodness." Kirstin nervously smoothed a hand down her blouse. "He's here."

"Who?"

"Shaw Harrington," Kirstin hissed. "Hedge fund extraordinaire and the founder of the Harrington Foundation."

Eviana glance down at her outfit. The bright yellow of her skirt suddenly seemed garish, the little flowers on her blouse childish.

"I'm sorry, Kirstin. I had on a suit and—"

"You look great." Kirstin gave her a look, one that told Eviana to not get so deep inside her head. "If he doesn't pick us because you're wearing a fantastic skirt, his loss."

Another knock sounded. Kirstin opened the door, but with the way the small space was angled, Eviana didn't get a glimpse of legendary Shaw Harrington.

"Good morning, Mr. Harrington. Thank you for coming to us."

"You're welcome."

Eviana froze.

There's no way...

"Ana?"

Kirstin glanced over her shoulder and gestured for Eviana to join her. "Mr. Harrington, I'd like for you to meet my intern, Miss Ana Barros."

Each step reverberated through her body as her heart sank in her chest. She knew even before Shaw Harrington came into view what he would look like, from the broad forehead and sharp blade of a nose to the dark blue eyes that widened a fraction as she came around the door.

His eyes flicked to hers, then fixed on her face. Shock flared for a single moment and then disappeared just as swiftly.

The man who had splashed her with rainwater, whom she had flirted with on the street, was her boss's potential new client.

Definitely not my best morning.

CHAPTER FOUR

Eviana

EMOTIONS TANGLED IN her chest, the strongest being nervousness that she had spoken so frankly and freely with a prospective client who apparently had the power to change the course of Kirstin's business.

Unsure if he would want their impromptu morning meeting revealed, she offered him a polite smile. "It's nice to meet you, Mr. Harrington."

He stared at her for a long moment, eyes narrowed, suspicion evident on his face.

"Good to see you again," he finally said with an emphasis on the last word.

Kirstin glanced between the two of them, concern deepening the slight wrinkles on her forehead. "Do you two know each other?"

"We met this morning at Braw Roasterie." Eviana kept her voice even, her tone pleasant. "Happenstance."

Shaw continued to watch her with that razor-sharp glint in his eye. She returned his stare with what Madeline teased her as her "resting royal face." Amiable yet devoid of any true emotion.

A princess never lets the world know what she's truly thinking.

That wasn't just one of Helena's rules. She'd heard them plenty over the years—from her father, from Nicholai, from well-meaning parliamentary members and public relations representatives. She'd hated it as a child. Yet at some point she had accepted it as the way things simply were and had done her best to keep herself contained. Hidden.

Coming to Edinburgh had been like waking up. Stretching her wings for the first time. It had been freeing to scrunch up her face when she'd tried a food she hadn't liked or laugh without thinking about how she might look on camera.

Slipping back into a role where she concealed her thoughts, even for just a moment, made her feel…uncomfortable. Self-conscious. Having that taste of freedom for the past eight weeks, the liberty to explore who she was and express herself without reservation, made putting that mask back on nearly unbearable.

But necessary. Whoever Shaw Harrington was, he was the ticket to Kirstin's success. Yes, this morning he'd relaxed for a few minutes. But he'd pulled back so quickly, retreated into that intense professionalism he was exuding now. An intensity that filled up the tiny office space and made Eviana feel like she couldn't catch her breath.

"Yes. Happenstance."

Muscles twisted and knotted in her back at the suspicion coating his words. She bit back a retort and fought to keep that serene smile on her face.

"It's a bit tight in here for three people," Kirstin finally said, even as she cast another worried glance between her potential new client and her intern. "I'll make us some tea, and we can have our meeting in the rooftop garden. Eviana, would you escort Mr. Harrington up there?"

Eviana grabbed her notebook, squared her shoulders and escorted Shaw out of the office and down the hall to the elevator.

"Fortuitous our meeting like that this morning," she said conversationally as she pressed the elevator button.

"Yes."

She glanced at him over her shoulder, then nearly flinched when she realized how close he was. A spicy, smoky scent wrapped around her, one that made her pulse beat just a tad faster.

"You sound suspicious."

"I am." He held up a hand as her eyes narrowed. "I'm the one who splashed you. I'm not thinking this is some devious campaign to get my business. It's just…odd. I wasn't expecting to see you again."

Surprised and, judging by his dark tone, not happy that circumstances had brought them together again. Whatever moment of camaraderie they had shared in the coffee shop had disappeared as soon as he'd made the decision to leave.

The elevator doors opened. Eviana stepped into the car, trying to ignore the ugly twist in her stomach as Shaw followed her and the doors shut. She'd talked with the man for less than ten minutes. She was leaving in four weeks. Oh, and he was about to be Kirstin's new client. Multiple reasons why she shouldn't be interested in him, why his easy ability to step back from whatever had passed between them shouldn't hurt.

But it did.

Later. She'd examine her feelings later. Right now, her personal views didn't matter. What did matter was doing whatever was in her power to land this contract for Kirstin and give something back to the woman who had taught her so much.

The doors opened. Eviana breathed in, unable to keep the smile from her face as she stepped out onto the rooftop garden. Crisp air greeted her, tinged with a hint of sea salt drifting in from the bay. Morning sun had chased away the gray clouds and left a spectacular blue sky overhead.

Whoever had arranged the garden had done phenomenal work. Golden-brown wood planks hosted flower beds teeming with orchids, wild thyme, bell heather and Scottish bluebells. White patio tables with matching chairs were arranged across the roof, providing little pockets of privacy for people to conduct business, along with a few picnic tables and lounge chairs for those seeking a break from the workday or a place to eat lunch in peace.

Or enjoy the view.

Edinburgh Castle stood proudly against the summer sky, over one thousand years of history behind those stone walls. It had been one of the things that had drawn Eviana to Edinburgh as she'd tried to decide where to take her sabbatical. It was somewhere new, somewhere far enough away that she could have a few blessed months of being just Ana. But there was that comforting familiarity in the winding cobblestone streets, the cry of a seagull, the castle on the hill. A blend of new and old.

"Have you visited the castle?"

Shaw's voice sounded just behind her. Invisible fingers squeezed her lungs as she tried to suck in a quick breath. She'd heard plenty of Scottish accents since she'd arrived in Edinburgh. When she'd first heard his voice, she'd thoroughly enjoyed the breathlessness the deep masculine tone had caused, the uptick in her heart rate.

But now it was a problem.

"I did my first week here. Hopefully I can go again before I return home."

"And when is that?"

Slowly, she turned. He was standing a few feet behind her. Plenty of space. But it might as well have been a few inches given the little electric pulses traveling through her veins.

"The end of July."

He blinked. "A month away."

"Yes."

He took a step closer. She stood her ground, threading her fingers together as she gazed at him like he was simply another human being and not a very attractive man wreaking havoc on her control.

"And where is home exactly?"

"Southeastern Europe."

There was that twitch again. The tiniest movement of his lips. The ache from earlier returned in full force. What on earth had happened to this man to make him put up such a stalwart front? To eschew something as simple as the pleasure of a smile?

"I want to reassure you, Mr. Harrington," she said, directing his attention away from any more personal questions, "that I will be able to maintain a professional attitude throughout your working relationship with Ms. Murray."

Even if I find you ridiculously attractive.

"Is there a reason why you wouldn't be able to?"

His cold tone shocked her out of her lingering attraction. Made it easy to move down the path of professionalism. The man might've looked like a god, but his personality was more like...

Helena.

She bit down on her lower lip hard. So hard she wondered if she'd drawn blood. But it was better than laughing out loud at Kirstin's potential new client.

Talk about an attraction killer.

"No." She inclined her head. "I just wanted to reassure you that my familiarity this morning is not how I conduct myself in a professional environment."

His eyes flickered over her face. For one pulse-pounding moment, she had the impression of Shaw looking past her mask. Of seeing the woman she truly was, the one who invited strangers to coffee and preferred living in a tiny apartment in Edinburgh.

The one who couldn't, or wouldn't, help lead her country.

She swallowed hard. His gaze moved down to her throat.

"Here we are!"

Eviana had never been so grateful for tea in all her life. Kirstin walked toward them with a silver tray in her hands, complete with three steaming mugs. They sat at a table near the railing. Eviana set her notebook on the table and pulled a pen out of her skirt pocket. Taking notes would help her focus on the job at hand and not on the man sitting less than a foot away.

A man who, despite his icy demeanor, saw far more than most.

"I was just briefing Eviana on your request when you knocked." Kirstin placed a mug in front of Shaw. "Let's start with you providing us with an overview of what brought you here."

Silence reigned. Slowly, Eviana looked up. Shaw was staring at the castle, shoulders tense, jaw firm, lips thinned into an angry line. At first glance, he looked furious. As if whatever circumstances that had brought him to Murray PR had also brought him to the edge of the control he seemed to prefer.

But the longer she looked, the more she saw. The shadows beneath his eyes spoke of restless nights. The faint frown between his eyebrows implied a deep-seated worry beneath the anger.

And as he turned his attention back to them, she saw grief in his gaze.

CHAPTER FIVE

Shaw

MORNING SUNLIGHT BATHED the sandstone walls of Edinburgh Castle. The walls blended into the cliffs beneath them, creating the illusion that the castle had been fashioned from the plateau that held it above the city.

Unreachable, unbreakable.

He had thought the same of himself. Yet the past few months had revealed that his self-image had been rooted in pride. Pride and a fixation on the end goal that had blinded him to the things happening around him.

Things like betrayal.

Out of the corner of his eye, he saw Ana look at him. He didn't see so much as feel her concern, as if she could sense his mood.

"Five years ago, I founded the Harrington Foundation."

In honor of my mother, he silently added.

For her. It had all been for her, for what they'd almost had and lost.

"I obtained a degree here in Edinburgh and attended graduate school in New York. My internship turned into a job at a hedge fund company. After my success in New York, I wanted to establish a fund that would support charities, specifically ones that focused on helping people become independent or overcome major challenges that upend normal life."

"The list of organizations you support is extensive."

Kirstin rattled off a list of charities in the United Kingdom and the States. Compared to the other two firms he'd met with, Kirstin was already demonstrating a level of knowledge that far exceeded the others. That he had reached out at eight o'clock last night and she was prepared just over twelve hours later was another mark in her favor.

He nodded in her direction. "Even though I resided in New York up until recently, when I founded the charity, I wanted it to first benefit the people in the city I spent most of my childhood in."

Except for those two years. Those two years when he'd thought that he and his mother had finally overcome, would never have to worry about putting food on the table or having a roof over their heads again.

"I created a board of trustees and turned over most operations to them, including the formation of a small marketing team and an accounting department. It was suggested that I continue to serve as CEO, but I am not what I would describe as a people person."

A slight noise sounded to his right. But when he glanced at Ana, her attention was focused on her notebook, her pen flying across the paper much as it had this morning in the coffee shop.

"I'm generally a private man. This makes it difficult for me to market the foundation and solicit the kind of donations we need to not only maintain but expand our operations. That's why I recommended they hire someone else."

Anger punched through him. Most days he could dismiss it, and on the rare occasion it rose up, he could usually control it. But there were moments like this, when the reality of the challenges he faced confronted him, that he struggled not to let it show.

"I recommended someone I met at Edinburgh University, Zachary White."

It was an accomplishment, he reminded himself, that he could say Zach's name out loud without letting his disdain show. A man he'd known had been spoiled and naive about the world beyond the gilded existence he'd grown up in as the son of a pharmaceutical developer. But still a man who had possessed the skills and affability Shaw did not. One who had made him believe he would do Shaw's vision proud.

Ana's pen continued to scratch across the paper.

Did she have any knowledge of what had happened? Had she heard the rumors? Did it change what she thought of him?

Stop. It didn't matter what Ana thought or didn't think. What mattered was, if he chose Murray PR, that she would do her job and do it well.

"Ten months ago, Zachary came to me. He wanted to expedite our fundraising by investing some of the foundation's funds. He wanted my opinion before presenting it to the board. It was a good idea, and it's not an uncommon practice among charities, but the investment he initially identified was questionable."

To say the least.

Shaw had barely had to glance at it to recognize it for what it had been: a scam.

"I encouraged him to speak with the board but to avoid that investment. Instead, he used his exceptional public-speaking skills and charm to persuade the board it was a good investment, then chose to sink half the foundation's funds instead of the five percent he'd been approved for into a hedge fund through an offshore account in the Cayman Islands." The anger seethed in his chest, pulsing in time with his heartbeat. "We lost over one million in savings, along with over two dozen donors who had made substantial gifts in the past two years, when the news broke."

He looked at Ana then. She didn't hesitate as she continued to write and take notes. Her face remained impassive, her demeanor tranquil despite the bombshells he had just dropped.

"Where does that leave you now?" Kirstin asked, redirecting his attention away from her intern.

"The investigation was completed on Wednesday. The board of trustees, the charity, and I have been found innocent."

Just saying the words out loud brought a much-needed sense of calm.

"Congratulations."

He nodded to Kirstin. "Thank you."

He, of course, had known all along that he'd had absolutely nothing to do with Zach's foolish investments. But to hear it stated in court, to have it on record that he had not been involved, had loosened a band wrapped around his chest. Had given him hope that perhaps things could still be salvaged.

"Zachary, on the other hand, is facing numerous charges. The trial, of course, won't happen for quite some time. But now that I've officially been cleared, I want to move forward with a campaign to entice our donors to reinstate their financial support."

"What is your primary goal?"

Ana's voice flowed over him, soft and soothing.

"The long-term goal is to reestablish our reputation and move past this. But in the short term, my primary goal is to reconnect with some of our highest-profile donors."

Or rather, he thought darkly, ex donors. The people who had withdrawn their support and fled as soon as the Harrington Foundation's name had been dragged through the mud by the worldwide press.

Part of him understood. As a hedge fund manager, he'd often made difficult decisions on where to invest and where not to invest. But the part that didn't, the man who had reviewed the lengthy list of commitments they wouldn't be able to fulfill without a quick return, was furious. The people who had kept the foundation afloat were extraordinarily wealthy—far wealthier than him. They owned private planes, numerous villas scattered around the world. They knew the work the foundation did, the people it helped start new chapters and get on their feet. It wasn't worth enough for them to stand up to the court of public opinion.

Which brought his fury full circle back to the one man who had caused it all. A man he had hand-selected based on hard facts and, over time, had even trusted to a certain extent.

This was what trust led to. Volatile emotions that impeded judgement. The tightness in Shaw's neck twisted harder and harder until he almost couldn't move.

"Not to be rude," Ana asked quietly, "but why

are you doing this? Why not a member of the board?"

"Given that they approved the investment, we all agreed it would be best for them to stay in the background for now. They're innocent—" a fact he'd had confirmed by an extensive private investigation of his own "—but they still made a mistake in not fully vetting Zachary's choice of investment, as well as not having safeguards in place to catch his mistake until it was too late."

Guilt pricked his conscience. The board had told him several times they'd been expanding too quickly, that they'd needed to slow down, hire more people, evaluate their procedures as they'd grown.

But he hadn't wanted to slow down. And now he was paying the price.

"The board also thought that as founder, I might be able to resurrect our reputation faster than a new hire, someone with no ties to the foundation."

Kirstin nodded. "Smart."

He gave her a tight smile. "Except the reason I declined the role of CEO in the first place is because I am not a people person. I don't converse well with strangers. I understand the board's thinking, but I'm concerned about the execution."

More like he anticipated complete and utter disaster unless he had a professional on the sidelines helping him through. Reaching out for help from a public relations firm was the last thing he'd wanted. Assuming they survived this, the foundation would be adding its own PR director, if not a small team.

But right now, he needed immediate action from someone who had experience with this sort of catastrophe. Someone like Kirstin Murray, who had worked for an international news organization in London for years before moving to Edinburgh and starting her own firm. A firm where she took on cases for small organizations. Even though the Harrington Foundation had been on an upward trajectory, they had a staff of fewer than two dozen people. The majority of operations were centered in Edinburgh.

If Kirstin could come up with a better campaign than some social media proposal like the last firm, one which included him making a video for Tik-Tok, he would hire her on the spot.

"What are your thoughts on connecting with the donors?" Kirstin asked.

"Something private."

His tone was firm and brooked no refusal. That was an area the first firm had failed on. They'd suggested gala fundraisers, giveaways, splashy events that would only draw more attention. Later, yes, when the foundation was back on its feet. But the last thing he needed right now was to have images of high-profile elites dancing and drinking as the foundation failed to send money to those in need.

"Like a private dinner."

Shaw glanced at Ana, then nodded at her suggestion. "Yes. Something where I can speak with them one-on-one, establish trust. Provide data and answer hard questions they may feel more comfortable asking without an audience."

Ana frowned slightly. "Data is great. But with something of this magnitude, you'll need to personalize it, too."

He gritted his teeth. "I know. That's why I'm here. I don't do personal."

She pressed her lips together as if she were trying to suppress a smile. When he narrowed his eyes at her, she ducked her head.

"Given what you've shared, I'm confident Ana and I can come up with a proposal to meet your needs." Kirstin smiled at him. "I can have it to you within two days."

"Tomorrow morning by eight."

Kirstin arched a brow as Ana's head came up. "Eight?"

He started to stand. "If it's not possible—"

"It is."

Surprised, he and Kirstin both looked at Ana. She glanced first at her boss, then at him, her chin raised, her expression determined.

"We can have a detailed proposal to you by eight tomorrow morning."

Kirstin's lips curved up with pride before she tilted her head to the side. "I agree. We just need the names of the donors who are your highest priority."

Shaw stared at them both for a long moment. Then he nodded. "I look forward to your proposal."

"Thank you. I'll walk you out," Kirstin offered as she held open the door.

Shaw gave Ana a brief nod as he left. She gave him that slight smile again, one that made him feel as if she'd grouped him in with the rest of the world and shut him out.

The notion burrowed under his skin and stayed there, an irritating itch that persisted down the hall.

"Your intern is very bold," he observed as they walked to the elevator.

"Don't let her fool you," Kirstin said with a fond smile. "She professes to be a novice, but she's a natural communicator. I've learned a lot from her as well. And," Kirstin added as the elevator doors opened, "I really believe with my experience and her insight, we can bring the foundation back on track."

As the doors slid shut and the elevator descended, Shaw let out a harsh breath. The thought of hosting a dinner, of trying to make friendly conversation as he worked to reassure some of the wealthiest people he knew to resume their donations left his body wound tight.

You'll need to personalize it, too.

A fist grabbed his heart, squeezed. Sharing his mother's story—his story—would no doubt entice some donors back.

Nausea curdled in his stomach. His mother had worked so hard, fought for so long to give him everything she could. She hadn't lived to see the success he had achieved. But everything he did, he did for her. For her memory. If honoring her meant pushing outside his comfort zone, then he would do it wholeheartedly.

But he refused to share her sacrifice.

Another image flashed into his mind. One of Ana seated at the table in the café, blond hair falling over her shoulder, that slight smile on her face. He'd vowed that morning to forget her, to not let one encounter upset his focus.

But now, as he walked out onto the sidewalk, he couldn't deny the flicker of interest that lingered, the desire to know more about the audacious young woman.

Except if you hire Murray PR, she'll essentially be your employee.

He shoved thoughts of her smile out of his head. Whether or not he hired Murray PR, he intended to stay as far away from Ana Barros as possible.

CHAPTER SIX

Eviana

A SHRILL PING yanked Eviana out of her much-needed sleep. She and Kirstin had stayed at the office until nearly nine o'clock perfecting the proposal Kirstin was going to deliver to Shaw Harrington. Due to Eviana's early wake-up call the previous morning, her mood was less than charitable toward her unknown caller.

Grumbling under her breath, she grabbed her phone and was about to decline the call when she saw the name on the screen.

"Kirstin?"

"Ana." Her boss's hoarse voice came through the line. "I'm so sorry to call you so early."

"No, don't be. What's wrong?"

"My mother…"

Cold fingers wrapped around Eviana's heart and squeezed. Kirstin's primary reason to move to Edinburgh and start her own firm had been to move in with her aging mother who was slowly losing her mobility. Eviana had never met her, but

Kirstin had frequently shown photos of them having in-home movie nights, dining at local restaurants or taking slow walks through Leith or along Portobello Beach.

"Kirstin…"

"She's alive."

Eviana's breath rushed out. "Thank goodness."

"But I don't know…" Kirstin's voice trailed off. "She fell overnight." Her voice caught, broke. "I slept right through it. I didn't find her until an hour ago."

"It's not your fault."

"But—"

"It's not," Eviana interrupted firmly. "You were with her. Who knows how much longer she may have gone without help if you hadn't been there for her?" She gentled her voice. "You love her, Kirstin. You're a good daughter."

Kirstin sucked in a shuddering sob. "Thank you, Ana."

"You're welcome. I'd feel the exact same way, but I'm not the one in the middle of this, so I can tell you you're doing far more than many would. Focus on your mom. Text me updates, but other than that I don't want you to worry about anything at work."

"I just…the Harrington Foundation proposal. I hate putting all of that on you."

Katastrofa.

Eviana scrunched her eyes tight. Of course.

Her resolve to keep Mr. Rich and Moody at arm's length was off to a rousing start.

"You're not putting this all on me." Did her voice sound normal? Like she wasn't inwardly cursing or her pulse hadn't shot up beyond a healthy limit? "You're taking care of your mother, which is where you need to be. And I'm stepping up to do the job you've been training me to do."

The words barely left her mouth before doubt flooded her veins. Hadn't she said similar words to her brother? If this was a bakery in Leith or a bookstore in the Grassmarket, she would have no problems. But was she capable of leading a project of this magnitude? Of working alongside a man who had captured her imagination even as he unsettled her with his coldness and intrusive perception?

Another muffled sob from Kirstin answered her unspoken questions. It didn't matter if she was capable or not. She would make this work.

"I won't let you down, Kirstin."

"I don't know what I'd do without you." Kirstin let out a deep, shuddering sigh. "Thank you, Ana."

Eviana sat there in bed for a solid minute after Kirstin had hung up, the phone in her hand as she stared at the wall.

The memory came back, stronger than yesterday. She could feel the paper beneath her fingers, the glossy folder underneath that held the speech written for her by someone else. Could still see the sentence that tripped her up. The one she'd stumbled over as the words had come out of her mouth because it had sounded nothing like her. There'd been so many gazes trained on her, watching her slow descent as heat had crept up her neck and pierced her skin to settle behind her eyes as she'd fought past the sudden lump in her throat.

She'd been sitting in a chair with a bottle of water in the reception room, trying to figure out what had happened, when she'd overheard Helena out in the hall.

This never happened with His Highness.

It didn't matter whether she'd been speaking of Nicholai or the late king. Neither of them had stumbled. Faltered.

Failed.

Why that speech? Why that event? Even now she couldn't pinpoint the reason why she'd slipped. The not knowing was the worst. When would it strike again?

Her fingers tightened around the phone. What if it happened with *him*? As she was trying to help her friend achieve her dream?

Panic flared. She closed her eyes, mentally reached out and wrapped her hands around it. Squelched it. She had failed before. But she'd learned a lot since. She was also unencumbered from the restrictions that had constantly made her question herself.

She would not fail now.

She glanced at the clock and sighed. Just after five thirty. She tossed back the covers, stood and stretched. She had to be at the Harrington Foundation office by eight, which meant she should aim for seven thirty in case of traffic or some other unforeseen event.

Like getting splashed by a hedge fund millionaire.

Really, she thought as she padded into the living room and pulled back the curtains, this was an opportunity. A chance to use what she'd learned working for Kirstin and couple it with the confidence she'd developed living as Ana. A confidence she hoped to somehow bring back with her to Kelna.

She wrapped her arms around her waist and watched the sun rise above the horizon. So many unknowns still lingered. Fear fluttered like trapped butterflies in her chest. But she also had resolve. Determination. A friend who needed her.

And a client who desperately needed her help.

Eviana turned away from the window and dove into what had become her morning routine. Opening curtains, putting the kettle on, doing a few stretches in the tiny living room. The four apartments on her floor would have fit into her bedroom at the palace back in Kelna. But she loved it, from the trio of curved windows that overlooked the street to the carved trim that separated the cream-colored walls from the ceiling. The faded coloring added to the historic charm. She loved making tea in the comfort of her kitchen, a room so small she could stretch out her arms and touch both rows of cabinets. No worries that someone would interrupt her precious alone time to whisk her away to yet another scheduled event.

Her head thumped against the cabinets as she leaned back against the counter. Was she capable of this? Could she be the princess her country needed her to be? That her brother and Madeline needed her to be?

She wouldn't go back on her promises. But *dragi Bože*, there were days when it felt impossible.

Eviana shook her head as she reached across the narrow space and pulled the teakettle out of the cupboard, then turned to the tiny sink to fill it. Right now, she needed to focus on the Harrington Foundation and how she was going to work with one very attractive, very cold-mannered millionaire. At least she'd proven to herself whatever attraction she'd experienced wasn't going to interfere with their working relationship. She'd slipped into "royal mode" easily once she'd realized he was a potential client. Years of training had made it second nature even if she despised the mask she wore.

There had been the added element, too, of not wanting to attract Shaw's attention. Not only was Shaw her potential client and therefore temporary employer, but she couldn't get involved with anyone. She'd made a mistake inviting him to coffee, yes. But engaging in an actual affair was one line she had not crossed.

Even, she admitted with a small grin as she placed the kettle on the stove, if she dreamed of it.

A pleasant warmth stirred in her belly at the memory of how he'd looked at her when she'd pitched her idea. When she'd first uttered the words "private dinner," she hadn't missed his body tensing, his eyes narrowing. But as she'd talked, the tension had eased, replaced by one of interest and respect.

She blew out a breath. Shaw was a man who noticed details, things out of place. He'd already heard her unfiltered. Letting small glimpses of her personality show through every now and then wouldn't be the end of the world. But the rapport and camaraderie she enjoyed with Kirstin would not be acceptable.

The teakettle started to whistle. She would do her job and do it well, seeing Shaw only when she had to and conducting herself professionally when she did.

Two hours later, Eviana walked into the glass-enclosed lobby of the Harrington Foundation. An elegant building with a stone facade, it hosted three levels of offices, meeting rooms and a conference room on the top floor next to Shaw's office.

She pressed the button for the elevator.

"Good morning, Miss Barros."

Warmth pooled in her belly as that deep, rough voice sounded just behind her. She turned slowly, giving her a few precious seconds to compose herself.

"Good morning, Mr. Harrington."

Once again, the man looked as if he'd stepped off the pages of a magazine. Navy suit with a matching vest and a black tie. His dark red hair was combed back again, not a strand out of place, as he stared down at her.

She resisted the urge to fidget with her own hair, wrapped in a tight bun at the base of her neck. But as Shaw continued to gaze at her, she had a frantic thought that he was peeling back the layers she'd carefully hidden behind, stripping her down until she had nothing left to hide behind.

Coward.

The thought had her raising her chin and straightening her shoulders.

Respect glinted in Shaw's eyes before he nodded to the elevator. "Going up?"

No, I was just admiring the elevator.

She bit back the dry reply and gave him a small smile. "Yes."

His eyes narrowed, but he stayed silent. The elevator doors opened a moment later, and they stepped in. Eviana breathed in deeply, a mistake she instantly regretted as Shaw's scent wrapped around her. Smoky wood and spice, hints of something wild that contrasted with his buttoned-up appearance.

"Kirstin texted me this morning and said she would not be able to attend the meeting," he said.

"I see."

Part of her almost wanted him to dismiss her, to tell her he had no interest in meeting with an unseasoned intern. It would make things so much simpler.

But that wouldn't be fair to Kirstin. And another part of her, the defiant part that rattled in the box she'd stuffed it into long ago, wanted to see this project through.

"Kirstin assures me that even though you're just an intern, you're immensely qualified to fill in for her and walk me through the proposal."

Eviana gritted her teeth. Yes, *just* an intern.

"I'll do my best, sir."

Silence fell between them, thankfully broken a few seconds later by the doors opening. Shaw gestured for her to exit first, then led her down a carpeted hall toward a gleaming wood door with a gold plate affixed to it.

Shaw Harrington, Founder.

The door swung open. Eviana's mouth dropped open. One wall was comprised entirely of glass. Less than a quarter of a mile away, the steep, craggy slopes of Castle Rock stood proudly over the city, topped by the majestic stone walls of Edinburgh Castle. She'd thought her view of the castle was incredible. But it was nothing compared to this.

She moved toward the windows, entranced. "How do you get any work done?"

"You get used to it after a while."

"I don't see how."

Shaw cleared his throat. Eviana turned, inwardly wincing as she yanked herself away from her daydreams. Another trait that separated her from her brother. Performing in public came easy to Nicholai, whereas she felt like she always had to be on guard, to ensure she was acting with propriety and decorum.

"I'm ready for your proposal, Miss Barros."

Her proposal. It might as well as have been, since she was presenting her and Kirstin's plan to the man who, as her boss had said, could make the future of Murray PR.

No pressure.

Eviana pulled a leather folder out of her messenger bag and handed it to Shaw before taking the seat across from his desk.

No pressure at all.

CHAPTER SEVEN

Eviana

"TELL ME ABOUT your proposal."

The butterflies flapped wildly in her chest. With one sudden push she was back on that stage. But instead of facing down over one hundred people, she was looking into just one pair of arctic blue eyes.

I will not fail. I will not fail.

"You'll begin with individual meetings with two of your donors who have suspended their contributions." She paused, inhaled quickly. "Roy Miles and Olivia Mahs. Your top two donors, and from what I found online, they have strong relationships with several other key donors.

"Meet with Roy and Olivia. Persuade them to renew their donations." As she spoke, her voice strengthened with conviction. "Then in three weeks' time, you will host a private dinner for a dozen donors who are no longer contributing to the foundation. Assuming Olivia and Roy agree to recommit, invite them to be a part of the dinner and serve as unofficial cohosts. Have them share why they decided to resume."

The man didn't even blink. "And after?"

She swallowed hard even as she kept her spine straight and her expression placid. He might not have been jumping up and down for joy, but at least he hadn't tossed her out.

Yet.

"It's going to take time." The words reminded her of the countless times she'd sat by hospital beds, holding hands and offering encouragement tempered with reality. It had been one of her favorite duties, the simple act of connecting with her people, of seeing them smile and supporting them through some of their most challenging times. A role she had loved, and one she drew on now as she continued. "But getting funds flowing back in while reestablishing trust is the first step. After you achieve that, then look ahead to hiring a new CEO, increasing public donations and investing in publicity once you have the support of your former donors. Their recommitment would be a huge selling point."

Shaw's lips tightened a fraction. "Given their faithlessness, I'm not holding my breath."

Eviana hesitated. "Since Zach was the primary link to those donors, it makes their withdrawal more understandable."

"Agree to disagree."

The man's words could have frozen hell. As a

princess, this would have been an occasion where she continued on, politely ignoring his breach of manners.

"You don't have to like it. But if you can't understand it, you'll struggle to convince them to come back."

Eviana blinked. *Did I really just say that?*

Apparently she had because Shaw sat back, his thick brows drawing together as he regarded her with curiosity. Curiosity, she noted, edged with irritation if his tense jaw was anything to go by. Few people probably dared to challenge him. But if he couldn't handle constructive feedback, then it didn't matter whether she was here with Kirstin or working alone. Murray PR was successful because Kirstin encouraged her clients to do hard work, not just strive for the perfect image with no substance underneath.

Eviana waited, hands folded in her lap, heart thumping.

"Acknowledged."

She barely kept her composure, fighting back a grin of triumph as she inclined her head to him. "Thank you."

"Did you summarize all of this?"

"It's all listed in the proposal," she added with a nod to the folder.

Shaw opened the folder and started to flip, reading each and every single page. Eviana sat as she had done so often in meetings, ceremonies, events where her mere presence had been the only requirement. That and not functioning, not doing anything that might invite criticism.

Twice Shaw glanced up, his eyes flicking to hers as if to gauge her level of irritation at his thoroughness. She simply smiled in return. Fifteen minutes was nothing compared to a four-hour military ceremony or the six-hour economic forum she had sat through last year to allow Nicholai to track down Madeline in Kansas City and properly propose.

At last, Shaw sat back in his chair. Even in a more relaxed pose, the perpetual tension gripping his body was evident in the taut tendons of his neck and the firm slash of his lips.

"I don't like special events."

Her heart sank. She'd botched it.

"However, I'm willing to make an exception with this proposal."

Elation surged through her. "Thank you."

"I'll expect you and Kirstin to start tomorrow."

"I'll be happy to start as soon as you need me. Kirstin…" Eviana paused. "With Kirstin's family emergency, I will be your primary contact for the next couple of days and—"

He sat forward in his chair, the action almost like a lunge with how quickly he moved. "I thought she was only detained for the meeting."

Eviana lifted her chin as irritation flickered

through her at his accusatory tone. "I'm telling you now before we begin any work."

The beat of silence that followed spoke volumes, as did the gathering anger in his eyes. "I understood her to only be gone today, not for the beginning of a campaign. An omission on both your parts that borders on a lie."

Eviana opened her mouth to retort, then stopped. Given what he had just gone through, she could understand his reaction. "I won't say I'm sorry if the alternative was you declining to meet with me in the first place knowing Kirstin would be unavailable at first. However, I will apologize if my actions hurt you in any way."

Shaw blinked in surprise. Then, he slowly leaned back in his chair. Fingers drummed on his arm rest once. Twice. "Apology accepted."

The words sounded almost wrenched from his chest. But he didn't strike her as the kind of man who normally accepted apologies.

"I have reservations," he said.

"Understandable."

"Is there any possibility of Kirstin returning in the next week or two?"

Again, Eviana hesitated. "I don't know. I'm happy to convey whatever information she's comfortable sharing. But as I referenced earlier, it's a family emergency, one that is ongoing."

The royal in her told her to stop there. But the friend in her, the passionate soul that had been allowed to thrive these past eight weeks, pressed forward.

"I will say I greatly admire Kirstin. Having the opportunity to work with someone like you is something she has been pursuing ever since she opened her firm. Yet when someone she loves needed her, she went." She nodded to the folder. "The proposal in front of you is the result of her nearly thirty years of experience in the field. Even though I would be the one to get it started, it's a plan created with her expertise and knowledge. And," Eviana added with a bravado she didn't feel, "she trusted me to carry on her vision."

Shaw slowly turned his head and gazed out the window at the castle. "Trust is not a commodity to be shared lightly. Or at all," he murmured so quietly she almost wondered if she imagined it.

"Anyone would hesitate after what happened."

"Even before Zach…" His voice trailed off, and he shook his head slightly. "I am making what is, at least for me, a very difficult decision."

Her lungs constricted. Had she misread him?

"Of the three firms I have consulted so far, yours is the only proposal that seems to have truly taken into account the situation and my personal requests for as much privacy as possible. I would like to hire Murray PR."

Eviana sat, frozen in her chair. Giddiness rose up inside her like a bubble about to burst. Finally, Kirstin would get the chance she deserved. And she had helped. Not just with the proposal, but with selling Murray PR's services to Shaw. Instead of backing down and following rules and protocols, she'd taken a leap of faith and relied on the confidence she'd been slowly building to advocate for the firm. A move that had paid off.

"You won't be disappointed," she said.

Shaw held up one finger. "I am throwing a clause into our agreement."

He could throw whatever he wanted to. Eviana was determined not to let this opportunity pass her by.

"If I am not satisfied with your performance at any point in the next two weeks, I will cancel the contract at no cost to myself or the foundation."

"I'll want to confirm that with Kirstin—"

"Yes or no. Right now, or the deal's off."

Pressure slammed into her as her confidence evaporated, insecurity and doubt quickly filling the vacuum. This should have been Kirstin's call. Eviana had no business making decisions of this magnitude.

Yet what other option was there?

"Miss Barros—"

"Done."

She'd talk to Kirstin later. If Kirstin disagreed, she'd wire for money from home to cover any penalties. She wouldn't have her friend pay for her mistakes.

That hint of a smirk played about his lips. "Let's hope you're not overly confident in your abilities."

Eviana inclined her head to him as she stood. She didn't like being backed into a corner by a man who thought he could simply order people about. She had met plenty of people like him.

But this was the first time she could deal with someone like him and do it on her terms. Another building block for her confidence.

"I'm not." She leaned into her frustration and resentment as she gave Shaw an uncharacteristically sharp smile. "I'm just realistic."

CHAPTER EIGHT

Shaw

"Mr. Harrington?"

Shaw glanced at the speaker on his desk. "Yes?"

"Miss Barros is here."

It had been three days since Ana had strode into his office with that serene calmness overlaying a spine of steel. The proposal had impressed him, as had Ana's alluring combination of confidence and sheer audacity.

The plan she and Kirstin had prepared was a good one. He'd thrown out his stipulation about her performance more as a challenge to see how she would respond. That she had taken him up on it without so much as batting an eyelid told him that while Miss Barros might've been an intern, she was either an exceptionally confident one or she had prior experience that made her overqualified for her current role.

Which begged the question, he thought as a knock sounded on his door, why was she interning for a small public relations firm? What had brought her here to Scotland?

"Come in."

His chest tightened as Ana walked in. Like the last meeting, she was wearing black pants, a white shirt and a black blazer. Almost identical to what she'd been wearing when he'd accidentally splashed her. A far cry from the colorful ensemble she had changed into. That bright yellow skirt had seemed more…her. She wore her suits well, with a grace and maturity that women far more experienced would envy. Yet it seemed…out of character. Like a colorful painting had been muted.

Good God, stop.

She was a woman, not a piece of art. And he was a man with a mission, not some smitten teenager. Ana had stayed true to her word and maintained a professional demeanor in every interaction they'd had. That he was struggling to keep a leash on his own errant thoughts clung like an irritating burr to his already shortened temper.

"Good morning, Mr. Harrington."

He dismissed the uptick in his pulse as her soft accent floated over him. "Miss Barros."

She slid a folder across his desk before sitting across from him. "Roy Miles has agreed to dinner. He has availability tonight, tomorrow and early next week before he and his wife leave for Kenya."

Shaw didn't bother to hide his scowl as he flipped open the folder. The foundation needed people like Roy. People who had grown up with wealth, who wallowed in it and were always looking for an excuse as to where to spend it.

But that was also the problem with people like Roy. They were capricious, full of their own importance and subject to random whims.

Just like Zach.

I did it for the foundation, he'd said.

No. Zach had done it for himself. He hadn't liked being told no, had been so convinced of his own superiority that he had plowed forward without thinking about how his actions would affect anyone else in his orbit.

"Where is this meeting taking place?"

"The Dome. Upscale restaurant, a staple of Edinburgh's dining scene. The kind of place that will impress Mr. Miles and has the added benefit of being a favorite of his wife's whenever they're in Scotland."

Shaw gave her a brief nod. Impressive. "What night are you free?"

Perhaps it was petty, a result of his own inability to stifle his attraction, but he couldn't help but enjoy the look of surprise on her face.

"Excuse me?"

"As I mentioned in my initial meeting with you and Kirstin, one of the things I struggle with is developing and maintaining personal relationships. I need someone with me as a sort of…"

"Buffer?"

"Exactly. Someone who can be on standby to assist, to add the personal touches that I struggle to exhibit."

A trait he had never regretted. Not until he had been confronted with the reality of how much he had come to depend upon Zach's affability.

"As I'm sure you're aware," he added with a pointed gaze, "many major organizations have their own public relations departments and representatives who accompany their executives to a variety of events to do exactly that. A gap in our current structure, but one we will eventually rectify."

Twin blooms of color appeared in Ana's cheeks. It was gratifying to see those touches of humanity in the woman who had ensnared him with her spontaneity and sunny outlook on life, only to retreat behind a bland mask.

"I am aware of the role many PR executives play."

She paused, her eyes flickering to the side. Was that fear on her face? Something uncomfortable twisted in Shaw's gut.

"Is everything all right, Miss Barros?"

Her attention jerked back to him. "Yes. I'm just surprised that with your concerns the other day about dealing with just an intern you would trust me with something of this magnitude."

He blinked, then struggled to suppress a smile. She had parroted his words with a formal primness that most would have mistaken for simply repeating what he'd said. But he didn't miss the flash of irritation in her eyes.

"I had concerns. You alleviated them enough for me to choose Murray PR. Until your boss is available, I expect you to fill in the roles she would have served in."

She sat there, staring at him.

"Is this no longer a suitable arrangement?"

He hadn't realized it was possible for her to sit up even straighter, but she did.

"No, Mr. Harrington. I'm just surprised. I'm free tomorrow."

"But not tonight?"

A slight frown drew her brows together. "I can make tonight work if you require it."

Jealousy unfurled in his chest, unexpected and heavy. "Do you have a date?"

"As I said, I can make tonight work if needed."

It should come as no surprise that a young, attractive, self-assured woman would have men interested in her. The fact that he loathed the idea as much as he did, however, was a knot he was not prepared to untangle.

"Tomorrow is fine," he said. "Please make sure to wear something formal."

"Of course."

"Give me your address, and I'll pick you up at seven."

"I'll catch a taxi," she said.

He glanced up. "I would prefer to pick you up."

Fire flashed in her eyes as her chin came up. "And I would prefer to take a taxi."

He sat back, steepling his fingers as he regarded her with a gaze that had made men twice his age quake in their boots back in New York. Ana, however, simply returned his stare. He shouldn't admire her show of strength. Zach had defied him, too, and look where that had led. Shaw had learned a valuable lesson—that while he might have kept himself impervious to personal relationships, he'd slipped when it came to professional ones. Had extended too much trust without even realizing it until it was too late.

"Why do you not want me to pick you up?" he asked.

"I like being in charge of myself."

Her answer seemed genuine, truthful. He was projecting his own experiences onto her. Memories of a time when he'd lied about his age to secure a job and help his mother pay the seemingly endless list of bills that kept them trapped in poverty.

His gaze darted to the photograph in the silver frame on the edge of his desk, angled so that only he could see it. Red corkscrew curls in a wild cloud about his mother's face. Her lips were parted in laughter, her blue eyes sparkling. A student photographer from the university had captured it on a rare day off when she'd taken him on a picnic to the park.

It was the only picture he had of her. If the office caught on fire, it would be the one thing he would save.

When he looked back up, Ana was watching him, curiosity on her face. Curiosity and a hint of empathy in her green gaze. An empathy he didn't want or need.

"While your personal preferences are noted, I will pick you up, Miss Barros. I will not be tethered to the irregularities of a taxi schedule," he said. "When I tell Mr. Miles and his wife that we will be there at seven, I want to ensure we'll be there at quarter till."

"Understood."

Her voice was polite. No change in her expression. But he could sense the disapproval, the irritation in her clipped movements as she pulled the pad of paper closer to her and jotted down an address.

"Do you have availability in the morning to review our strategy?" she asked.

"See my secretary on the way out. She'll schedule you."

He turned his attention to his computer screen. He was being rude. But the longer she stayed in his office, the more he wanted to turn the picture around, to show her the woman who had fought tooth and nail to provide him with a better life. Who was the heart and soul of the Harrington Foundation and everything he was trying to achieve.

But he didn't.

"Goodbye, Mr. Harrington."

His fingers tightened on his computer mouse. He stared at his screen until the words blurred and he heard the click of the door closing. Murray PR had been the right choice. In the two meetings he'd had with Ana, she'd proven to be everything Kirstin had said.

She wasn't the problem. He was.

He stood and stepped to his window. He'd grown up with Edinburgh Castle standing guard over the city. Over time, it had become one of those symbols he barely glanced at. It was always there, would always be there, at least for his lifetime.

As he stared at the stone walls, the stalwart cliffs holding up hundreds of years of history, he saw it through Ana's eyes. The tradition, the majesty. He envied her outlook on life, her ability to appreciate the little things he so often missed as he marched forward, so determined on where he was going he often forgot to look around at where he was.

He turned away and moved back to his desk. Yes, life would be better if it were all sunshine and rainbows. But he'd grown up in the real world, one where he had known hunger and cold and judgment. His mother had been a constant blessing that many in his position had not had. It was because of her that he had become successful, that he was now in a position to help others. He would not lose sight of that purpose, not for anything.

Or anyone.

CHAPTER NINE

Eviana

EVIANA SMOOTHED HER hands down her skirt as she stared at her reflection in the full-length mirror. She had attended balls, weddings and a slew of formal dinners ever since she'd been five years old.

She had never felt more nervous than she did right this moment.

The black dress she had chosen, a Gucci gown with a full skirt, square neckline and straps tied off in tiny bows at the shoulders, was a little much for a supposed intern. But in her mind, it was worth the risk. Not only for Murray PR, but for representing the Harrington Foundation and clearing this first hurdle.

If there was a small part of her that hoped that Shaw would be impressed, so be it.

She tucked a blond strand back into place. It had been over two months since her bodyguard, Jodi, had suggested she dye her hair to give herself even more freedom of movement. That, along with the bangs across her forehead, had so far done its job. Not that many people in Scotland had even heard of Kelna or its royal family. But it still gave her a degree of comfort, a safety net that allowed her to move about Edinburgh as if she were truly just a civilian living her life.

She sighed. To date, Jodi's presence had been comforting, a reminder that she had someone here who knew her deepest, darkest secrets and would do anything to protect her. But tonight it made her feel…false. A reminder that she was living her own odd version of a fairy tale. One that would soon end.

Her phone buzzed, drawing her out of her reverie. When she saw Shaw's name on the screen, her heart leapt into her throat.

Three minutes away.

Their meeting this morning had gone well. Almost perfect. She had laid out the key talking points she thought might persuade a man like Roy Miles to resume his donations. Shaw had agreed to all of them and delivered a couple of practice speeches for her to review. Much better than yesterday's face-off over him picking her up, she thought with an irritated tug on one of the bows at her shoulders. Although the meeting today had been frustrating in a different sort of way. As Shaw had gone over talking points with her, he'd impressed her with his depth of knowledge, the dedication he felt for the work the foundation did.

A sigh escaped. The man wasn't just a spoiled millionaire playing around with charities. Beneath that seemingly impassive exterior beat a passionate heart. It was subtle. One had to realize that Shaw Harrington was not just a cold block of ice to even identify the signs.

It would be so much easier, she thought as she snatched her shawl and clutch off a chair, *if he was simply a jerk*.

Easier to ignore the attraction that had resurfaced with those glimpses of the man behind the mask. The deepening of his voice, the softening around his eyes as he spoke of the Harrington Foundation and the work it did. The pride in his voice as he mentioned the success rate of a charity in Inverness that helped low-income families receive paid job training.

She shook her head as she headed toward the door. Instead of mooning over him, she needed to think like a professional—how best to use those glimpses to further the cause of the foundation. If she could just help people see that side of him, share whatever it was that drove him to work so hard, the donors would come back, arguing over who got to pledge the most money.

But for whatever reason, he wouldn't. Which was why she was here.

Her phone dinged again. She glanced down at her screen and smiled.

Good luck tonight!

Kirstin had checked in regularly, offering insight and suggestions to the plan as she went along. With her mother moving from the hospital back into her home but still needing help moving around their apartment, Kirstin had been far too busy to return to work. She had called and had an extensive conversation with Shaw this afternoon, too. All Kirstin had said was that it had gone well, that Shaw had been very understanding regarding her mother and he had reported being pleased with Eviana's work.

Which was good because even though she'd seen a bit more humanity today, he was not the type of man to give praise lightly or converse in a friendly manner. Although, she conceded as she locked the door to her flat and started down the stairs, it had been a good test of her ability to continue working in a tough environment.

A smile lit her face as she stepped out onto the stoop. She'd persevered. Instead of constantly being on edge, evaluating her every move, she'd simply focused on her work. If doubt crept in or if her gaze had occasionally strayed to Shaw's handsome profile, she'd pushed through.

Tonight would be a good night. Not only a potential milestone for the foundation and Murray PR, but a personal one, too. A test of the work she'd done, both to develop as a professional and to personally overcome her lingering insecurities.

A far cry from helping to run a country. But each step was progress.

Her phone dinged a third time. Her smile disappeared as she saw the name.

Nicholai.

Slowly, she tapped the screen.

Hey. Hope you're enjoying your sabbatical. It'll be good to have you home.

She stood there, staring down at her phone as she fought against an onslaught of emotion. She missed her brother. Missed Madeline. Her country, the people who had supported and loved the royal family through thick and thin.

But there was grief, too, the kind of grief that came from knowing when she returned home, it would never be the same.

And beneath it all—the pain, the loss, the confusion—lay the worst emotion of all: fear. She hadn't even lasted a year with her new duties before the worst had happened. One failure might be excused, especially given her father's recent passing. But what if it happened again? Two more times? How many times before she not only lost faith in herself but her people did, too?

"Ana."

Her head snapped up. She'd been so caught up in her own miserable musings that she'd missed the black car pulling up to the curb.

And missed Shaw getting out of the car.

Warmth spread through her. Dressed to perfection in a black tuxedo and crisp white shirt, his beard had been trimmed and his hair combed back to showcase the angular planes of his face.

But it wasn't just his attractiveness that caught her attention. No, it was the glimmer of worry in his eyes as he moved towards her.

"Are you all right?"

Royal smile.

"Yes." She slid her phone into her clutch. "Just a text from home that surprised me."

Acutely aware of his gaze on her, she descended the stairs with slow steps.

"I'm fine."

If he had accepted her casual dismissal of the moment, it would have been so easy to move on with the night. But instead Shaw leaned forward, his intensity magnified tenfold as he directed it squarely at her.

"Sometimes the most painful things are the small things. They rear their head when you least expect them."

Her throat closed. She didn't want this man to understand her on such a deep level. To understand her unlike anyone else ever had.

And yet, she thought as she met his stare, *he does*.

"My father passed away last year. This trip has been valuable in so many ways. But it's also been an escape. Just thinking about going back home is…" She paused, trying to find the right word. "Hard." Her voice broke. Not much, but enough to convey the depths of her grief.

Instead of stepping back or chastising her, Shaw's gaze softened even further. "It's never easy."

"No. It's not."

She broke eye contact and glanced around the street, taking a moment to compose herself and mentally letting go of the tension Nicholai's text had ushered in.

"Thank you for listening."

Shaw nodded as his features relaxed and he gestured toward the car. At some point during their conversation, a chauffeur had gotten out and stood guard by the passenger door. But as he reached for the door handle, Shaw waved him aside. He opened the back door and gestured for Eviana to climb inside.

As she moved forward, Shaw held out his hand. She took it, partially out of habit, partially out of instinct.

Their fingers brushed. The world shuddered. Stopped. Such a simple contact, similar to the graze of fingers when she'd handed him his coffee days ago. Except this time, his hand wrapped around hers, a firm, comforting weight that sent tendrils of warmth through her body. Her breath caught in her throat. She looked down at his hand engulfing hers, then slowly raised her gaze. Shaw stared at her. Aside from the warm pressure of his hand on hers, he was so still he could have passed for a statue.

"Hvala vam."

It took a moment for her to realize she had thanked him in Croatian. Flustered, she climbed into the limo. His hand tightened on hers for a heartbeat.

And then he released her without a word.

The limo ride was quiet, tension pulsing between them like a living thing. Eviana kept her eyes trained on the passing scenery. Normally she would enjoy the sights, the stone architecture, the gardens and green spaces dotted throughout the city.

But she saw nothing, registered no details as the limo moved through the night. All she could think about was the man sitting opposite her. The man who was essentially her boss, who held her friend and mentor's fate in his hands. Who prized honesty and despised any type of deception. If Kirstin ever found out Eviana's identity, she would be shocked, yes, but would probably also find it fun, an adventure of sorts having a princess work for her. If Shaw found out, however...

Eviana suppressed a shudder. At the very least, he would cancel the contract with Murray PR. For a man who claimed to have little ability at building and maintaining relationships, he made her want to confide in him, to show him the woman she was.

But it wasn't meant to be, she firmly reminded herself as the limo pulled up outside the restaurant. While he might've felt something similar to what she was experiencing, his fury at her deception would eclipse any attraction.

The chauffeur opened the door, and Shaw got out. Even if he could get past her real identity, there was the matter of...well, everything else. Everything about her life, her real life, was the antithesis of what Shaw wanted for himself. Public scrutiny, constant demands on her time. The man she married would have to accept her duty to the crown and be accepted by the people of Kelna.

Shaw extended a hand to her. She mentally braced, then placed her hand in his. She'd maintained walls her entire life. Whatever spell she had fallen under when it came to Shaw Harrington needed to be broken and broken fast—before she made a mistake that would hurt her friend or herself.

Or both.

CHAPTER TEN

Shaw

WINEGLASSES CLINKED INSIDE the cavernous space of the Dome's main dining room. Curtains trimmed in gold brocade shut out the night and created an intimate atmosphere despite the numerous tables arranged throughout the room. Chandeliers gleamed overhead as waiters moved around the tables, carrying silver trays laden with caviar, brisket and Scotch pie.

Across the table, Roy Miles tossed back a hundred-pound glass of whisky like he was at a London rave instead of an upscale restaurant.

"Excellent choice," Roy repeated for the fourth time.

At just over fifty years old, he kept a trim physique and skin bronzed to such a degree it hinted at help from a tanning salon. His suit was from Savile Row, his watch a Rolex.

Shaw understood, at least to some extent, investing in quality. The clothes he wore, the car he drove—all of it was an investment. The clients he worked with trusted someone who gave off a certain appearance. The same could be said of the people who donated thousands to the Harrington Foundation. Quality made an impression.

But Roy was also a prime example of how money could be wasted.

Shaw forced what he hoped looked like a smile onto his face as he held up his own glass of whisky that he had been nursing for the past twenty minutes.

"Thank you."

Roy's wife, Victoria, was engaged in a quiet conversation with Ana. The two had hit it off almost as soon as Shaw and Ana had walked into the restaurant. How Roy had ended up with a woman like Victoria, a retired veterinarian with silver-blond hair wrapped into a simple braid and a kind smile that reminded Shaw of his mother, was a mystery.

But Roy had also been one of the most prolific donors to the Harrington Foundation, eager to have his name attached to what he'd seen as a rising star in charity work. That Zach had met Roy at some celebrity event in New York City and plastered Roy's photo across the foundation's social media and brochures had no doubt helped.

Unfortunately, Roy's obsession with status did not mesh well with the fallout from Zach's choices.

"How's business?"

Not the most engaging question Shaw could

ask, but it was at least an attempt to engage with
Roy instead of point-blank asking him to resume
his donations. Out of the corner of his eye, he saw
Ana glance at him and give him a slight encouraging nod before returning her attention to Victoria.

He'd never relied on the approval of others. But
the small acknowledgment soothed some of the
restless energy coursing through him.

"Excellent," Roy boomed. "The wife and I just
bought a ranch in Montana."

Shaw tried, and failed, to keep the frown off
his face. "A ranch?"

"Yep." Roy raised his hand to signal the waiter
for another glass. "Four hundred acres set against
the Rocky Mountains. I forget how many cattle.
And a four-thousand-square-foot ranch house
complete with its own sauna and hot tub."

"Dear," Victoria said with a patient smile on
her face, "let's not brag."

"Let's!" Roy shot her a toothy smile. "How many
times have I told you I thought I would make an
excellent cowboy?"

"Plenty," she replied dryly.

"Perhaps to you, but not to these two lovely
people."

Shaw's hand tightened around his glass. The
audacity of the man to sit there, to brag about
his spending even as charities floundered to support people desperately in need, made him want

to toss the contents of his very pricey drink into Roy Miles's face.

"Congratulations." Judging by the warning look Ana shot him, his voice had come out just as growly as he'd intended.

"Thank you." A waiter set another glass of whiskey in front of Roy. "As much as I'm enjoying this dinner, you didn't just ask me here to lavish food on me."

Finally.

"The investigation has officially concluded in New York." Shaw tempered his voice, strove for professionalism and confidence. "The Harrington Foundation, the board and I have all been cleared of any wrongdoing."

Roy didn't even look at him, choosing instead to survey the array of Scottish cheeses on the platter in the middle of the table.

"Given that we are no longer under suspicion," Shaw continued as he focused on a point over Roy's shoulder instead of the irritating man himself, "I wanted to ask you to consider resuming your donations to the Harrington Foundation."

Roy used a fork to spear a piece of brie. "I'm glad to hear you've been cleared, not that I had any doubts. But it's all—" he waved his fork in the air and nearly sent the cheese sailing across the dining room "—so recent. I know your group does good work. I admire that. It's why I donated in the first place."

You donated because Zach sold you on the idea of being a knight in shining armor, come to save people beneath you.

"But I'd like to give it a little bit longer," Roy said just before he popped the piece of cheese into his mouth. "Let things die down a little more. Let's revisit this in a few months."

It was a wonder Shaw didn't break the glass in hand.

Ana and Victoria had stopped talking, their attention now fixed on Shaw and Roy. Victoria sent her husband a narrow-eyed look. But Roy's attention was focused on spooning a generous amount of caviar onto his beef. Each motion ratcheted up Shaw's simmering anger.

"Have you thought that being the first donor to renew his donations might make its own statement?"

Ana's serene voice floated over the table. Roy glanced at her, then smiled, his eyes warming with appreciation at her beauty.

Shaw's anger heightened as it twisted into an ugly mass inside his chest. Ana looked lovely, yes. Stunning. When he'd seen her on the stoop of her apartment building, strands of curling blond hair framing her heart-shaped face and wearing a dress that looked tailor-made to her petite figure, he hadn't even bothered to excuse away the surge of attraction.

So he could understand other men looking, too.

But not the way Roy was, like she was a prize to be won.

Ana's eyes flickered to Shaw. The tiniest shake of her head made him forcibly relax, mentally unwinding each muscle as he sat back in his chair. He didn't want to trust her, didn't want to turn things over to her completely.

But until he got himself under control, he had no choice.

Roy's avaricious leer disappeared as his expression turned thoughtful. "Can't say I thought of it that way."

"The Harrington Foundation continues to do good work."

Ana spoke gently but firmly, a blend that Shaw envied. It reminded him of Zach in that she spoke as if she'd been with the foundation for years instead of just a few days. But whereas Zach had relied on a blindingly white smile and charm, Ana radiated quiet authenticity.

"Even with the lack of funds," she said, "they've continued to make substantial contributions and support as many charities as they can."

Shaw forced himself to sit still and let her do what he had hired her to do. Roy was giving her more eye contact in the last thirty seconds than he had given Shaw in the past ten minutes. It was a struggle to turn things over to her, to not interfere. But trust issues or not, he knew his own weaknesses. And he was coming to learn more about Ana's strengths. Strengths he both envied and admired.

"Worthy efforts, Miss Barros. But," Roy said, his eyes flicking to Shaw before refocusing on Ana, "I lost a lot of money when this thing blew up. So did associates I recommended the Harrington Foundation to. We thought we knew Zach White. We trusted him." He faced Shaw then, his eyes suddenly hard, all traces of the partying buffoon gone. "I don't know you, Shaw Harrington. No one does. Learning that that donation was lost is not something I'm going to get over easily."

"Zach is gone." Shaw's voice whipped out over the table. "That will not happen again."

"How do I know that?" Shaw didn't give Roy any ground even as the older man leaned forward and pointed a finger at him. "You want us to trust you, trust your foundation, but you've given us nothing except some statistics to smooth over what happened."

"Mr. Harrington is an honorable man."

Shaw's head snapped around at Ana's voice.

What on earth is she doing?

"I know you don't know Mr. Harrington well, but the fact that he believed in something so much that he invested, and continues to invest..."

Her voice trailed off as her gaze collided with Shaw's. It was more shock and fury that kept him mute. How had she found out about his investments? Worse, how many times had he told

Ana over the past few days that he preferred his privacy? That he wanted to persuade the donors based on the merits of the foundation and not his personal life?

Ana cleared her throat. "That he continues to invest his own funds speaks volumes."

Her last words fell flat, her confidence gone. Shaw knew he'd taken a bad situation and made it worse with his reaction. But he couldn't see past the betrayal. A minor incident compared to Zach's treachery, but a betrayal nonetheless. His ongoing donations would be a matter of public record, including the sizable chunk he had invested six months ago. But she hadn't asked his permission to share that detail, had gone against his specifications for privacy.

Roy glanced between Shaw and Ana with renewed interest even as Shaw's blood curdled in his veins. This was what he hated—being looked at like a specimen, being the center of attention. Once a small detail was revealed, people wanted more. They wanted to dig deeper and deeper until they had the whole story of how Shaw Harrington had grown up in the slums of Edinburgh, bouncing from place to place while his mother had worked herself to death trying to provide for them. How he'd used his own money to start the foundation and do what another charity had failed to do for him so long ago.

His lips curled into a slight sneer. The perfect

sob story. One that, if Ana continued to share these little tidbits, would eventually be revealed. The thought of having his mother's sacrifices used as marketing fodder cranked up the heat on his simmering anger and turned it into a fire that burned away any remaining patience. He'd trusted Ana for all of five minutes, and she'd gone rogue in less than three. No matter how the rest of this hellish night proceeded, he would either make his conditions crystal clear with no more second chances. Better yet, maybe he should fire Murray PR and be done with Ana altogether.

"Something to consider, Miss Barros. Now," Roy said as he picked up his fork and knife again, "tell me more about yourself, my dear. Are you enjoying your time in Scotland?"

Ana glanced at Shaw as if to confirm that he wanted her to follow Roy's lead and drop the conversation. For the first time since he'd met her, worry gleamed in her eyes. Uncertainty drifted across her face. Something twisted in his chest at causing her discomfort. It twisted even tighter at the thought of having to fire her.

And then he dismissed his ridiculous emotions. Feelings had no place in business.

He managed to make it through the rest of the meal, mostly because Roy did the majority of the talking. Finally, after what had to have been the longest hour of Shaw's life, Roy stood and leaned across the table.

"Thanks for the meal, Shaw. I'll be in touch."

I doubt that.

Shaw acknowledged Roy's statement with a nod of his head. Victoria was much friendlier, coming around the table to offer him a hug. She did the same to Ana, whispering something into her ear and giving her a light squeeze on the arm before following her husband out of the restaurant.

Shaw sat back and watched as a waitress cleared the remnants of their meal. Ana, who had been mostly silent since her attempts to salvage the pitch, kept her gaze focused on her glass of wine until the waitress left.

"What was that?"

To her credit she didn't flinch, even though he flung the words at her with the force of an arrow whistling toward its target.

"Me trying to persuade a client."

His discomfort returned, along with a heavy dose of guilt that beat its fists against his defenses. It only made him angrier, as did her refusal to meet his gaze.

"No." Shaw leaned forward and placed one hand on the table, his fingertips pressing down into the tablecloth. "That was you violating a direct order not to share any private information."

Her head snapped up. He barely resisted moving back from the sparkling fury in her eyes.

"No, it was me doing the job you said you would trust me to do." She leaned in, closing the distance between them as her confidence returned in full force. "I didn't share anything that's not public knowledge."

"It might be available to the public," he growled back, "but that doesn't mean I want it bandied about. At what point did you forget my specific request for privacy?"

She set her wineglass down so hard the ruby liquid swirled dangerously close to the rim.

"On the first charge, not only are your donations a matter of public record, but it was included in a statement from *your* foundation to the press three months ago."

Cold flooded his veins. "What?"

Ana pulled out her phone, tapped something on the screen and handed it to him. Shaw read through the article, his body tensing as he got to the last paragraph.

Shaw Harrington is committed to maintaining the foundation and keeping it solvent throughout this crisis. Mr. Harrington has donated a significant portion of his own funds to cover as much of the deficit as possible for the current operating year.

"I didn't approve this."

He glanced at the date, then bit back a curse. He remembered that day. It was the day Zachary had shown up to his office in New York. The week before Shaw had decided to rent out his penthouse and return to Edinburgh for the foreseeable future. Zach had managed to bluster his way past the secretary on the first floor, but Shaw had alerted security before he'd made it off the elevator. The guards had hauled him away as he had shouted out Shaw's name. The image of Zach being tossed out of his office had made its rounds on social media in the evening news. Shaw had told his marketing department to handle the subsequent press.

"I didn't know."

The excuse sounded lame even to his ears.

"I shared information I thought you had already approved. And," she added as she leaned forward once more, color high in her cheeks, "this is the kind of information that makes a difference, that changes someone's mind. You heard what Roy said—you can't do it solely on the basis of what the foundation does. Not anymore. Not after their trust has been broken."

"You don't think I know that?"

Heads turned their way as his voice rose above the din. One woman with dark blond hair in a long braid and dressed in a simple black suit seemed to take an especially strong interest in their conversation as she stared at him over her shoulder. She turned away when he glared at her.

"This is not the time or place for this conversation," he said.

"Obviously." Ana stood and tossed her napkin

onto the table with an uncharacteristic lack of finesse. "Although I will say this, Mr. Harrington—you're asking these people to trust you, yet you trust no one but yourself. I don't know how you expect to make any headway when all you're offering is a one-way street on your own terms. Oh," she added with a sweet smile laced with daggers, "and in case you forgot, you hired a *public* relations firm. Something to keep in mind if we proceed."

The truth of her statement punched him in the gut. He gritted his teeth, consciously aware of the heads still turned in their direction. "We can continue this discussion in the car."

Ana paused, then looked down her nose at him. "No."

Blood roared in his ears as she continued to look down at him as if he'd been the one to do something wrong. As if she were the boss, not him.

"Excuse me?" The two words sounded as if they'd been pulled through a steel grater.

"I said no. You didn't trust me to do my job tonight." She held up a hand as his lips parted on a retort. "Yes, I faltered. But that was after you interfered. Had you not, I might have been able to make more progress with Mr. Miles." She grabbed her shawl off the back of the chair. "Now, if you'll excuse me, I would prefer to discuss this in the morning once we both have the chance to cool off."

Before Shaw could respond, Ana turned and walked out the door. He nearly followed her. But he didn't. Following would be a sign of weakness, chasing her down when he was the one who had hired her. He might give her a second chance, one he didn't extend to many. Knowing how she had gotten the information about his donations helped ease some of his anger. But she still should have talked to him, cleared it before she'd gone off script.

"Would you care for another drink, sir?"

Shaw looked up at the waitress, then down at his nearly empty whisky glass. "Tempting, but no, thank you. Just the check."

Slowly, everyone else returned to their meals, leaving Shaw alone at the table.

Usually he preferred it this way—no one to depend on but himself. But as he glanced once more at the door Ana had walked out of, he didn't feel strong.

He just felt alone.

CHAPTER ELEVEN

Eviana

EVIANA WALKED OUT of the restaurant, each step heavier than the last. But she pushed through. She didn't want to see Shaw, couldn't bear to let him see the swirl of emotions spinning inside her chest like a cyclone. Embarrassment, anger, frustration.

And above all, fear. Fear that the last nine weeks had been nothing more than slapping a bandage over the fact that she wasn't capable of being the kind of leader her brother was, the kind of leader their father had been. Leaders who exhibited diplomacy and confidence, who didn't let angry glances and self-doubts prevent them from doing what needed to be done.

Of all the nights to let her heart speak instead of her head.

Her phone vibrated in her pocket. She pulled it out, her stomach sinking when she saw Kirstin's name on the screen.

How's it going? Can't wait to hear all about it. Still going to be out for a few days at least, but I know you're representing Murray PR well!

Eviana swallowed against the sudden thickness in her throat. Instead of doing well, she might have just torpedoed the entire contract by jumping into the verbal fray instead of doing what Helena had always encouraged her to do.

Sit. Observe. Be quiet.

Roy, for all of his bluster, had proven to be a far shrewder individual than she had expected. She'd observed him all evening, taken in by his obsession with fine whisky and high-priced food.

But when push had come to shove, Roy had shoved back. Hard. It had been challenging to sit off to the side and watch Shaw struggle to connect with the man.

She had met plenty of men like Roy before. Parliamentary members, CEOs from the companies trying to court Kelna's growing business and shipping sectors, dignitaries. Shaw was confident in what his foundation had to offer. But he certainly had not been lying when he'd said he struggled to showcase the personal side of the Harrington Foundation. To accept his role, even if it was temporary, as the face of the foundation.

Yet she had also seen other details, ones she had grown adept at noticing in her years of sitting on the sidelines. The way Shaw's eyes had followed the spoon as Roy had dumped caviar onto his plate, almost as if he'd been mentally calculating how much each spoonful cost, weighing it against the financial need of the people his foundation supported.

Shaw might not have been the most personable man. But he was certainly an honorable one. Roy had a point, yes. It was his money and his choice as to where to invest it. She had struggled with whether or not she should speak up, say something.

And then she'd remembered that this was the kind of role that she would be called upon to fill again and again in the coming years. She would have to speak up, even when she was unsure, even when she wasn't confident what the right thing to say was.

At first, when Roy had turned his attention to her and Shaw had remained quiet as she'd spoken, she'd felt brave. Confident. Feelings that had evaporated when she'd seen Shaw's face harden, felt the walls slam into place. Eviana had wanted to pursue her conversation with Roy, to share some of the facts and statistics she had compiled that demonstrated the true impact the Harrington Foundation had had over the past five years. That and the ongoing challenges since the fallout over Zachary White's fraud. Challenges that had left hundreds, if not thousands, of people struggling to make ends meet.

Irritation swelled. She'd been doing the right

thing. Roy had been listening to her—maybe not on the verge of changing his mind in that exact moment, but certainly closer than he had been with Shaw making stilted conversation and failing to contain his glower. But the fury in Shaw's eyes when she had met his gaze had made the words dry up in her mouth.

The rest of the dinner had been just as awkward and humiliating. She'd sat there like a rock, questioning every other word she'd come up with. All her hard-won confidence gone in the blink of an eye.

Or rather, she thought mutinously as she moved down the sidewalk, in one glare from a controlling millionaire.

A breeze blew down the street and whipped an errant curl across her face. She brushed it aside, the cool air soothing some of her ire. Unfortunately, that left her with the fact that even though Shaw had overreacted, she had failed at her job. Shaw had told her multiple times he didn't do well in those types of situations.

Embarrassment pulled at her limbs, crept under her skin and slid through her veins with an icy coldness as words from the past flickered in her mind.

This never happened with His Highness.

"Excuse me?"

A small voice sounded from a dark doorway to her right. She squinted. A young woman shuffled out, a stained blanket wrapped around her shoulders.

"Could you spare some change?"

Eviana smiled gently at her as she reached into her clutch. "I can. What's your name?"

"Catherine."

The girl's eyes were clear but nervous as her gaze darted around.

"What are you doing out here?"

Eviana held out several bills. Catherine's eyes widened.

"Lost my job. Left my boyfriend."

"I'm sorry."

"Don't be." Catherine grinned as she accepted the money. "He liked to smack me around, and my boss was a nut job."

"Then congratulations." Eviana paused. "There's a shelter near here. One that offers clean beds for a night."

The young woman's nose scrunched up. "I don't want charity."

"Not a charity. Just a place to rest while you get back on your feet."

Catherine tilted her head to the side. "Yeah. Maybe."

"Something to think about," Eviana said gently. "Have a good night."

She'd only made it a dozen feet or so down the sidewalk when she heard her name.

"Miss Barros!"

She turned her head as a car pulled up. Her heart dropped at the familiar leering grin of Roy Miles as he pulled a cherry-red BMW convertible up to the curb. Victoria offered her a wan smile from the passenger seat.

"Mr. Miles."

He beckoned for her to approach the car.

Will this night never end?

"A word of advice. There's a significant number of homeless in Edinburgh. Some of them need help. But the city has ample shelters to help them." Roy's eyes flickered toward the doorway behind Eviana. "If you give handouts to everyone you see, you're going to go broke very quickly."

Eviana's eyes moved from the Rolex watch on Roy's wrist to the gleaming polish of his convertible. She focused on those details as she fought against the rising tide of anger. Not just anger at this odious man and his utter lack of empathy, but years of standing on the sidelines, watching every word she said and never stepping up for anyone lest she make a bad impression.

Not anymore.

"Mr. Miles," she said, "I gave that girl twenty pounds."

"Which is kind, but—"

"Your Highland Wagyu beef with caviar cost nearly four hundred pounds."

Roy reared back, his expression hardening. "How I choose to spend my money—"

"Yes, I know and respect your ability to make your own choices." *Even if you are a colossal donkey.* "Just as I'm asking you to respect my choice. There are weeks where I have spent double and even triple the amount I just gave that girl on coffee. On coffee," she repeated, not bothering to hide her disdain. A disdain for not only him but herself as she reality of what she was saying hit hard. Of how she had judged this man even as she'd engaged in similar actions. "I would be lying if I said I gave money to every single person I saw. But if I feel drawn to do so, I will."

Eviana started to walk off, then stopped. *Might as well go all in.* She turned and folded her hands demurely in front of her as she arched a regal brow. "Those shelters you mentioned? Two of them are partially funded by the Harrington Foundation."

Before he could respond, she turned around again, intent on walking away and putting as much distance between her and Roy Miles and Shaw Harrington and the whole mess as possible. Hard to do when she ran right into somebody standing just behind her.

"Oh, excuse me…"

Her voice trailed off. Shock rooted her to the spot, swiftly followed by horror. Shaw stood in front of her, hands tucked into his pockets, watching her with an unreadable expression.

If he hadn't intended to fire her after their exchange back in the restaurant, it was a certainty now after the way she'd spoken to one of his top two donors.

Behind her, she heard Roy's car take off down the road, leaving her alone with one ticked-off millionaire.

"I suppose you heard that exchange."

"Most of it." Bland tone, blank expression. No clues as to what he was thinking.

She looked up at the sky and shook her head. "What are the odds?"

"The odds of what?"

Even though she would have preferred to crawl into a hole, she lowered her chin and met his gaze. "The odds of me finally saying something that needed to be said and you walk out and hear most of it."

He tilted his head to one side. "Do you think I don't approve?"

She threw her hands up. "I don't know what to think, Mr. Harrington. You hire me, tell me that yes, trust is hard for you but you think I'm capable of doing the job that needs to be done. Then, the very first time I try, you're furious. And that was just over sharing one small detail that was public information released by *your* organization. Essentially telling one of your largest donors that he's acting like a dobber isn't what most public relations professionals would do."

One corner of his mouth twitched. "Dobber?"

She narrowed her eyes. "Are you laughing at me?"

"I don't laugh."

She snorted. God, Helena would have a fit if she could see Eviana now. "That I can believe. One of the many words I picked up from Kirstin."

"I didn't hear you expressly call him that."

"I was thinking it," she retorted as she looked down at her watch. All she wanted was to get home and under the scalding hot spray of a shower. For the first time in weeks, she craved her suite back in Kelna. The marble Jacuzzi tub with its trio of bay windows overlooking the palace gardens that provided a partial glimpse of the sea. A place of refuge. One she had sought numerous times, especially over the past year.

"Look, I need to get going if I'm going to catch a bus—"

"Let me give you a lift."

She pinched the bridge of her nose. "Shaw, I don't want to talk anymore tonight."

Eviana could feel it coming on, that heaviness pressing on her, wrapping around her like a stranglehold. She could fight it. Would fight it. But it would be so much easier if Shaw wasn't there, watching her struggle with an unseen weight he couldn't even begin to fathom.

"Not talk. Just a ride."

She glanced down at her phone. Waiting for the bus would take at least five minutes, and that was assuming it was on time. The ride would be another thirty. Walking would easily put her at forty-five minutes to an hour. Riding with Shaw, however, would get her home in less than fifteen.

A sigh of defeat escaped her lips. "All right."

The chauffeur brought the car around. Shaw opened the door and she slid in, sinking into the depths of the heated leather seat. She leaned her head against the window and watched the buildings of Edinburgh pass by once more. The silence between them lasted all the way to her apartment.

At last, the car pulled up in front of her building.

"I'll walk you to the door," he said.

"It's not a date, Mr. Harrington." She didn't even care that she sounded snappish. It was like a dam had burst and she was no longer capable of maintaining any sort of pretense.

"No." Shaw rapped once on the glass partition between the front and back seats, then opened the door himself. "But it's the right thing to do."

Her hand slid off her own door handle as she forced herself to wait for him to circle around the car. She didn't want him to be nice to her. It was so much harder when he was kind, when he let her see those bits and pieces of who she suspected he really was.

He opened the door. Sensation still danced in her belly, but she was prepared this time to accept the hand he offered. True to his word, he walked her up the stairs to the front stoop as she pulled her key out of her clutch.

"My office, tomorrow, nine o'clock."

She nodded. Whatever the consequences were from her actions tonight, from her failed attempt to sway Roy Miles to renew his donations to being caught speaking in an unprofessional manner, she would handle whatever came her way with diplomacy and maturity.

"Nine o'clock," she repeated softly.

Shaw stared down at her. The longer he looked, the more her exhaustion melted away. A fluttering sensation flared, deepened, transforming into an awareness that made her lightheaded. His gaze moved down to her lips. She leaned forward, just a fraction, but enough to break whatever spell had settled between them as Shaw took a deliberate step back.

Mortified, she turned away as she jammed the key into the lock and twisted.

"Ana—"

"I'm sorry."

She walked into the hall and turned to close the door behind her. Shaw brought his forearm up and planted it against the door.

"Ana."

She looked down, unable to bring herself to meet his gaze. "Don't. I—"

"I'm sorry."

Her head jerked up. "What? I—"

"That was unprofessional of me."

She sucked in a shuddering breath. "I didn't exactly respond in a professional manner myself."

"It won't happen again."

A protest rose to her lips, then died just as quickly. He was right. It couldn't happen again. For so many reasons, ones she had repeated to herself multiple times over the past few days.

The true question she needed to ask herself, if he didn't choose to fire her in the morning for insubordination, was if she would be able to separate these personal feelings from the work she had promised to do.

"I know," she said. "And I... I won't..."

"I know."

It was too dark to tell what emotion flickered in his eyes. Surely it couldn't be regret. A man like Shaw didn't strike her as someone who regretted things very often. He made decisions and stuck by them. She envied him that certainty, that ability to move forward without constantly questioning himself.

"Good night, Miss Barros."

The coldness spread and wrapped chilled fingers around her heart.

"Good night, Mr. Harrington."

She closed the door and locked it, the sound of the dead bolt turning echoing in the empty hallway.

CHAPTER TWELVE

Eviana

EVIANA ENTERED THE ELEVATOR, a cortado in one hand and a black coffee in the other. The heat from the cups warmed her fingers. If only it could take away the chill that still clung to her after a night of tossing and turning.

She'd wanted to call Madeline. Tell her everything, from the failed meeting to that dreadful moment when she'd revealed the depth of her attraction to Shaw as she'd swayed towards him… only to be rejected.

Not just rejected, she thought as she barely resisted the urge to tap her foot against the floor, but rejected *nicely*. Why couldn't Shaw have been his usual brooding, borderline rude self? Why did he have to be kind in a moment of complete and utter humiliation?

Madeline would have made it into a joke. Offered words of encouragement and commiserated with all the goings on in Edinburgh. It had been a shock to realize how little interaction Eviana had

had over the years with people other than palace employees, her father and her brother. She'd considered the people she'd worked with for the hospital charity friends. But once she'd gotten to know Madeline, she'd realized she'd never had a true friend, one she could share absolutely anything and everything with without fear of rejection or judgment.

But that would be placing a great pressure on her future sister-in-law. Madeline wouldn't tell Nicholai where Eviana was and what she was doing if Eviana asked it of her. But putting her in that position, especially as she shouldered some of the duties Eviana had left behind for her sabbatical, would be unfair.

So instead, Eviana had taken a steaming-hot shower and sipped a cup of tea with a dash of honey just before lying down. She'd gotten some sleep but had been awoken around 2:00 a.m. by a racing heart and a highlights reel of her most embarrassing moments from the day flashing through her head. It had taken an hour of rolling this way and that, giving her pillow a few solid punches, and finally reading a few chapters of a mystery book she'd picked up to get back to sleep.

The elevator doors slid open, revealing the long hallway leading down to Shaw's door. She caught a glance of herself in a gilded mirror hanging on the wall and grimaced. The dark moons beneath her eyes stood out even more against her pale blond hair. She'd applied a heavier hand with makeup to make herself look at least somewhat awake. Her movements had been slow and sluggish as she'd pulled on her usual black blazer, black pants and a white shirt.

Better than a zombie, she comforted herself as she continued on. *Barely, but better.*

At least she'd left a little time for a coffee stop. The first sip of her cortado had steadied her somewhat, a liquid refresher to bolster her before she faced her judgment.

She stopped outside Shaw's door, sucked in a breath as she conjured up an image of steel doors slamming shut on last night with her stupid crush locked firmly behind them.

Dramatic, much?

One more deep breath. Then she knocked twice. Footsteps sounded behind the door. Her pulse started to pound as the door swung open. Dressed in his usual three-piece suit, this one a charcoal gray with a black tie that made him look every inch the imposing hedge fund manager he was, Shaw gave her a nod.

"Good morning."

At least he wasn't firing her before she even crossed the threshold.

"Good morning, Mr. Harrington." She held out the coffee. "A peace offering."

Shaw glanced down at the coffee. His lips

curved. Had she walked into an alternative universe by mistake?

"Thank you. Come in."

Still confused by his almost smile, it took her a moment to register what was on his desk. A cup of coffee with Braw Roasterie's logo on it and a smaller cup with the same design.

"Is that for me?"

"Yes."

She tried, and failed, to hold back her own smile. "Great minds." The tension in her shoulders eased as she sat down across his desk. This was good. Casual conversation. No fluttering in her chest, no warmth pooling in her stomach. "I guess I didn't convert you to cortados."

"I enjoyed the taste. But I've had a cup of black coffee every morning ever since I started university. It's a hard habit to get rid of. And the cortado…" His dark red brows drew together "It's rich. Indulgent."

"And you don't like to indulge?"

Dovraga.

She bit her bottom lip as the temperature of the room changed in an instant. Tension charged the air between them as their gazes met, held. The same flare of emotion she'd seen last night appeared in the dark blue depths of his eyes. But just like last night, he was still in control. His lips parted, no doubt to once again negate whatever was happening between them.

No. Now was the time to show both herself and Shaw she could keep things professional, too.

"My brother prefers his coffee black as well." She gave him a small, bland smile. "A touch bitter for my tastes."

Shaw's eyes narrowed. She met his gaze, striving for serene and unaffected as she waited.

At last, he nodded. "I spend money on some of the nicer things in life." He circled around his desk and sat. "I would be lying if I said I don't enjoy my home here in Edinburgh or driving a Rolls-Royce. But the clothes I wear and the car I drive serve a purpose. The people I work with, and the people I'm trying to work with," he added dryly, "respond to quality. To someone they think is like them."

Implying Shaw wasn't from their world. When she and Kirstin had researched his background in preparation for their proposal, there hadn't been much available on public record before he had enrolled at the University of Edinburgh for a finance degree. Given his preference for privacy, she hadn't bothered to dig further.

But now, as he sat there wearing his tailored suit as if he'd been born in it, a dominating force in his quietly luxurious surroundings, curiosity rippled through her. Who had Shaw been before he'd become a financial prodigy? What had driven him to create the Harrington Foundation?

"Are you not like them?" she asked quietly.

Darkness flickered in his eyes. "No."

The finality of the word told her that line of conversation was closed.

"Perhaps you should try a mocha, then. Coffee with just a bit of milk, sugar and cocoa powder. A touch of sweet, but not too extravagant."

His teeth flashed white as he let out a quiet laugh. The sound rumbled through her. For one moment, she saw him without the lines of tension in his forehead, without the weight he seemed to carry everywhere.

"Maybe one day." The smile disappeared as his face smoothed out. "Let's get last night out of the way."

Her shoulders tightened as she resisted the urge to shift in her chair. "All right."

"While I would still prefer to keep my life private, having read the article and better understanding where you got the information, I realize now that I overreacted."

Of all the things she had anticipated, acknowledgment of his own reaction had not been one of them.

"Thank you."

His eyes flicked once more to the picture frame on the corner of his desk. "When Zach made his choice to invest the funds, I didn't just lose an employee, I lost one of the biggest assets the foundation had. Zach made everyone feel like they were important, part of a mission."

Her heart ached for the trace of loss she heard in his voice. Even if he didn't want to admit it, she suspected that Shaw had thought of Zach as an acquaintance. Perhaps even a friend. Having one's trust broken was hard enough. Having it shredded by someone close hurt ten times worse.

"Zach choosing to 'make his mark' on the foundation, and his own ego without thinking through the ramifications of his decisions, has made it even more challenging for me to trust. And if I don't fix this," he added quietly, "even more people will suffer."

"You could hire a permanent PR rep now to—"

"No." He uttered the word firmly. "Eventually. But right now, I need to be the one to fix this. The Harrington Foundation is something I've been working toward ever since…"

A long moment passed. His brows knit together as if he were waging some internal battle. And then, slowly, Shaw reached out, picked up the frame and handed it to her. Eviana's breath caught as she stared down at the picture of the woman, at the joy radiating from her mega-watt smile, the familiar blue eyes and elegant features.

"Your mother," she breathed.

"She's the reason. For everything."

Eviana continued to stare at the photograph. She had so few memories of her own mother. But the few she did included laughter. Choosing the Kelna National Hospital as her first and primary charity had been because of her mother and the care they had given the late queen in her final days. Just those few years of memories had driven her. Understanding Shaw's motivation, even without the details of his life before, answered so many questions.

"How long has she been gone?"

"Twenty years," he said.

Her throat tightened. "My mother passed away twenty-one years ago."

When she looked up and their gazes met again, the arc that passed between them was not one of forbidden attraction but of shared grief. A bond she wouldn't wish on anyone else, but one that held some measure of comfort in knowing that she wasn't alone.

"You told me last night that people need a reason." He let a harsh exhale escape. "My mother worked herself to death. I don't want to exploit her sacrifice or her death for money. But I hope this provides some perspective on the importance of what we're doing."

She focused on the woman in the picture. Better than looking at Shaw and letting him see the emotion that must've been in her eyes. Heartache for what he must have suffered. Admiration for what he had done with his life. And tenderness for this newest layer he'd chosen to share with her.

Again, she had to remind herself, he hadn't shared that detail with her because of any sort of affection. It had been to help her understand the Harrington Foundation better. To help understand him and the kind of support he needed from an employee as he navigated a crisis.

Steel doors.

She pictured that warm glowing ball of tenderness, then envisioned throwing it behind the doors and locking them.

"Thank you." Eviana handed the picture back. "It does help to understand. I will verify any personal information in the future." She folded her hands together as she forced out the next words. "I also owe you an apology. While Roy Miles can be pretentious, the way I responded to him outside the Dome was unprofessional."

"Strong, perhaps," Shaw said with a shrug. "But I didn't find it unprofessional."

She blinked in surprise. "What?"

"I didn't hear everything Roy said. But I saw you give money to that woman. Based on your response and what I know of the man, I can only imagine what words of wisdom he tried to offer." He frowned. "If he had not been such a large donor, I would be divesting all ties with him. But what I heard was you stating facts, connecting the current situation to Roy's choice not to resume donations. Holding people accountable for their actions is not a bad thing."

"No," Eviana agreed. "I just sometimes struggle

to find the balance of maintaining a professional facade and finding the right words."

"You didn't seem to have any trouble finding the words last night when you confronted Roy. Trust yourself more."

Eviana's eyes grew hot. "Back home…my family encourages a more sedate response."

"As I've stated, I'm not the best example of diplomacy." He regarded her for a long moment. "The moments where you let go of that mask you wear or you just let the words flow instead of thinking about everything you're saying beforehand…that's the PR pro I want to work with."

Eviana arched a brow, a casual action that hopefully covered how much of an impact his words had. How much they meant to her when almost everyone else in her life told her to prioritize propriety over her own instincts.

"Really? Because I could have sworn you were going to drag me out of that restaurant last night if I shared anything else you found inappropriate."

"I have some work to do," he acknowledged with a small smirk. "Had I let you continue, who knows where things might have ended with Roy. Which brings me to my last point. I'd like to continue working with you and Murray PR."

He held out his hand. Relief nearly made her sag in her chair.

"And I would like to continue to represent both Murray PR and the Harrington Foundation." She shook his hand, satisfied when she felt only the tiniest spark.

"Even though Roy did not commit to resuming his donations, last night was a good learning experience." Gears in her mind started to turn, puzzle pieces falling into place as she slipped back into work mode.

"It was," he said. "And we have another opportunity to try again. The other donor you identified, Olivia Mahs, has agreed to meet with us in London in two days."

"Olivia Mahs. The railroad heiress."

Shaw nodded in approval. "Yes. She's only in town for twenty-four hours for a meeting."

"Kirstin told me to focus exclusively on the foundation for the next couple of weeks, so I can make that work." Excitement trickled through her. Her one and only trip to London had left her with a feeling of whiplash as she'd been whisked from one royal event to another.

"Excellent. I'd also like for you to write up some scenarios."

"Scenarios?" Eviana repeated.

"Yes. Practice runs, so to speak, so I'm more prepared to engage with Miss Mahs."

"I think that's a great idea."

"Good." Shaw held up two slips of paper. "We'll have plenty of time to practice because Miss Mahs has generously provided us with train tickets to London."

"Train tickets?"

"Yes. She's in charge of launching a new passenger line that specializes in luxury train travel. A return to the olden days, if you will."

An image filled Eviana's mind of a train moving along a track curving through green pastures fluffy clouds of smoke puffed from its chimney. A peaceful sigh slipped past her lips. "I've never been on a train before."

"It'll be just under five hours. We leave the day after tomorrow at nine a.m. and should arrive just before two. Olivia gave us a three-hour window that day between five and eight. I'd like for you to make the arrangements as to where we meet."

"Done."

This part of the job was her favorite. Finding out what motivated people and what mattered to them, then tailoring a meeting that spoke to them, drew them in. Something that made an impact and encouraged them to volunteer, donate or engage.

"And then the scenarios, questions I should anticipate as well as what you think will help me be more personable," he said.

Eviana glanced at the picture frame, now back in its original place. Part of her wanted to ask Shaw to reconsider his stance on sharing the foundation's origins. Perhaps there was a way to rephrase it, to focus on his experiences while keeping his mother's name out of it.

But she would honor his wishes. He was trying

to do better, and he had trusted her with a vulnerable piece of himself. A piece she suspected he rarely shared with anyone.

No, she would find other ways to put them at ease and let a little bit of his personality come through without placing him under a microscope. Knowing Shaw trusted her skills and even preferred the woman she had grown into these last couple of months made her feel seen. Confident. As if the shackles she had grown used to wearing had suddenly been ripped away and she could move with the same kind of freedom she had tasted working for Kirstin.

"We won't fail this time," she said.

"Ana." The subtle warmth in his voice froze her in place. "You didn't fail last night."

She didn't look up. Didn't want to see any sort of compassion, grace or other kindness that would make it that much harder to keep the doors shut on that infernal attraction.

"I appreciate the reprieve, but I disagree. Roy didn't agree to resume donations." She cleared her throat as she wrote something nonsensical in her notebook to at least give the appearance she was working instead of trying to resist her own foolish heart.

"Not yet. But you got through to him when I didn't. That wouldn't have happened if you hadn't been there."

Eviana waited a moment before glancing up. Thankfully he had refocused on his computer.

The worst thing about this man was that he moved through life all power and control and then out of the blue, he gifted her with words that touched on her deepest fears, soothed them, made her feel as though she could truly do this. Not just help the Harrington Foundation reestablish itself, but become a leader, someone Nicholai and Madeline and her people could depend upon.

Shaw Harrington was a dangerous man. The more she got to know him, the more she felt herself slipping down a dangerous slope. One she suspected that if she fell too far would result in her leaving broken pieces of her heart in Edinburgh.

CHAPTER THIRTEEN

Shaw

TREES AND GRASSY hills dotted with fuzzy sheep whipped past as the train sped through the Scottish countryside. It hadn't been more than a few months ago that Shaw had taken a train to London. On that trip, he'd spent most of his time on his computer, sifting through emails, evaluating reports from New York and, as always, monitoring media coverage on the foundation.

But today, as dark clouds scuttled across the sky and colored the landscape with shadows, he found himself looking out the window more and more. Noticing things he had missed, like the little stone cottage covered in ivy or the elegant manor house with horses grazing in the fields.

Although, he admitted as he tried to contain a small smile, Ana drawing his attention to various landmarks helped.

They were in the dining car, he with his laptop and she with her notebook. Her pen flew across the page, except for when something drew her attention out the window. Which seemed to be every three to four minutes.

Surprisingly, he didn't mind. In those moments when she looked out the window, he stole glances of her uniquely beautiful face that, every now and then, felt familiar. Something had changed for him the night of the dinner at the Dome. When he'd gone outside to wait for his car and seen her talking with Roy, his anger had propelled him down the sidewalk. Not just anger at her for continuing what he'd assumed was the earlier conversation without him present, but for the way Roy had looked at her just as he had the four-hundred-pound-an-ounce caviar.

But when he'd drawn close enough in time to hear her unleash her tirade against Roy, he'd stopped. What had transpired next had shot through his armor and left him defenseless long enough for his attraction to deepen. The proper professional he'd worked with for the past few days had vanished. In her place had been a stunning woman, fire and passion, who had taken a stand on someone else's behalf. Someone like his mother. Someone like him, or who he had been long ago.

As if that hadn't been enough, that moment on her front stoop had turned simmering warmth into a craving he'd nearly succumbed to.

Pulling back from kissing her had been the last thing he'd wanted to do. Which was why he had done it. He would not cross a line with someone who worked for him. But it had hurt, physically hurt, to see that embarrassment on her face. When she had shown up the next morning, the pressure that had tightened his chest as he'd walked away from her the night before had loosened.

She hadn't brought up their near kiss, so neither had he. Yet it lingered in his mind. Flared at the most inopportune moments. She appeared to have moved on once again quite easily. But he couldn't. Not with the memory of her voice vibrating with anger as she'd laid Roy Miles flat with her honest words. Not with the yearning that had shone in her eyes as their breaths had mingled in the summer air. The woman who intrigued him, the professional who impressed him and the fighter who surprised him had melded together until he couldn't ignore her or his own growing interest.

He could lie to himself and say he had shown her his mother's picture as a gesture of goodwill. But after hearing her defense of someone Roy had dismissed, her last words reminding Roy of the work the Harrington Foundation did, Shaw had wanted to show her his mother's picture. Give her a glimpse of why it all mattered.

Ana might have thought she'd hidden her reaction well. But he hadn't missed the tightening of her fingers on the frame, the slight bob in her throat as she'd swallowed hard or the lingering glimmer in her eyes when she handed the picture back. That his divulgence had impacted her had been yet another blow to the walls he'd kept in place for so long.

Shaw watched out of the corner of his eye as she hailed a passing waitress to ask about the teas on the menu. Enthusiasm buoyed her tone. A genuine smile lit her eyes and made her gestures more animated. Just like that first morning when they'd met.

She continued to remain secretive about her background, but given his own penchant for privacy, he had no room to judge. Still, the questions lingered, grew as he spent more time with her. Where did Ana live? What family drama had spurred her to leave Southeastern Europe and come all this way? Was there a man in her life back home?

The last question twisted his stomach into a knot. Nothing could happen between them. Even if circumstances hadn't made a relationship between them forbidden, could he even open himself up the way a woman like Ana deserved? Trust someone with the darkest parts of himself?

A year ago, the answer would have been a resounding no. He enjoyed dating when his schedule allowed for it. He'd had a couple of relationships that lasted a few months, even reached a one-year anniversary with a prosecuting attorney in New York. But all of his relationships had run their course. Agreeable affairs that had ended amicably. He'd entered into each one knowing there was an expiration date.

But now, as he watched Ana, the thought of her returning home in a few weeks made the landscape outside seem even darker.

The waitress came back with a teapot colored dark blue and decorated with gold filigree and two matching cups. She set both on the table, dropped a sachet of tea leaves into one and poured. Steam rose as the fragrant scents of lavender and mint floated in the air. The waitress set the other cup in front of him.

"None for me, thanks."

The waitress smiled. "No, sir, the lady ordered you coffee, black. I'll be just a moment."

His eyes flickered to Ana. She didn't notice his glance as she raised the cup up, her eyes drifting shut as she inhaled. A serene smile curved her lips.

It struck him suddenly that out of the few relationships he had had, none of his previous partners had bought him coffee. A minor detail, one that seemed inconsequential. Yet in the span of a week, Ana had bought him coffee multiple times. She was an intern, living in a decent townhouse apartment, but nothing compared to his home in Edinburgh's elegant Greenhill neighborhood. While Kirstin had struck him as a fair boss, she was still building her own firm. Chances were she wasn't paying Ana much.

But Ana had spent some of those hard-earned pounds on him.

Her eyes fluttered open. Her expression didn't change, but a rose hue tinted her cheeks. She glanced out the window.

"Oh, look!" Her teeth flashed white as she pointed to a sprawling stone estate in the distance. "A castle."

"Yes. Another castle," he said dryly.

She rolled her eyes even if she shot him a teasing smile. "I know you have the luxury of seeing a castle every single day you go to work, but in a month, I won't get to see architecture like this anymore."

His jaw tightened as he forced himself to remain outwardly impassive. "Are you excited to go home?"

She looked down at her tea. "Yes and no. There are things I miss. People, like my brother and his fiancée."

"When are they getting married?"

"October. I'm the maid of honor."

"A role you want, or one you were forced into?"

She chuckled. "Very much wanted. Mad, my soon-to-be sister-in-law, is the sister I never had. And she's made my brother very happy."

He noted the hesitation, along with the genuine happiness she seemed to feel about her brother's upcoming marriage. He wanted to ask more, wanted an explanation for the secrecy.

Yet how could he demand more information when he was unwilling to give answers of his own?

Telling her about his mother, letting her hold the photograph, had been one of the hardest things he had done in recent memory, aside from giving the order to have Zach thrown out of his office in New York. Zach and a couple close acquaintances knew he had been raised by his mother and that she had passed a long time ago. But as he racked his brain, he couldn't think of a single person he had told the role his mother and his upbringing had had on his decision to develop the Harrington Foundation.

No one he had wanted to confide in.

Ana set her cup down and reached for her folder. "How about we run through a scenario?"

That was the last thing he wanted to do. No, he wanted to sit and listen to the bits and pieces of herself she was willing to share. Hear the melody of her voice, her excitement at a random sheep or hills covered in purple blooms.

"All right."

She flipped through her notebook.

"Have you thought about getting a computer?" he asked.

"Oh, I have one. I just like pen and paper." Her fingers flipped through the pages with practiced efficiency.

"Why?"

"It makes me slow down. Think. When I have a computer in front of me, it's so easy to let it do all the work." She shrugged. "Pen and paper feels more...me. Ah, here it is." She looked up and gave him a challenging smirk. "Ready?"

No. "Yes."

The first few questions were easy, standard ones about the foundation, the work it did, how the board of trustees chose what charities and individuals to give grants to. All standard information on the foundation's website. But as they walked through each of his answers, Ana made moderate tweaks to each one. Small changes that didn't change the essence of what he said but added strength and personability.

"What happened with the Veach investment fraud?"

The question came out of nowhere, a sharp departure from what she had been asking. But she'd done it on purpose, to throw him off guard, just as Olivia or anyone else might. He respected her for it, admired her calm presence. If she'd been nervous to ask the question, it didn't show.

"It's difficult to talk about." He paused.

"No, that's good. You don't have to share everything," Ana said quietly. "But even just that little touch of humanity and honesty shows me some of the man behind the foundation."

He gave her a quick nod. "Zachary White served the Harrington Foundation for five years. In that time, he did good work. Unfortunately, six months ago he made the choice to invest half of the foundation's assets into the Veach Fund. It was marketed as a real estate investment opportunity. It was a scam."

He could still remember Zach showing up in his doorway, white as a sheet, hands shaking as he'd closed the door behind him.

I need to tell you something.

It hadn't just been that Zach had disobeyed his order to not invest. No, it had been the betrayal. The realization that, unintentional or not, Zach had been the closest thing he'd had to a friend in his entire adult life.

"Zachary's actions were...foolish."

"Foolish or criminal?"

He narrowed his eyes at Ana, but she didn't back down.

"Foolish." He released a harsh breath. "But not criminal. While Zachary made a poor choice, and one that went against my wishes, his intention was to find a rapid way to expand the foundation's wealth and increase the number of organizations we were supporting."

"Does that absolve him of blame?"

"No." He heard the rigidity in his voice, the temper. Paused and collected himself. "His intention, however good, caused significant losses. That's why the Harrington Foundation released

Zach from his contract the day he told us what happened."

"How will the Harrington Foundation…" Her voice trailed off as she peered at him. "Let's take a break."

"One more."

She looked as if she wanted to argue, but she obliged and glanced down at her notes.

"How will the Harrington Foundation ensure something like this will never happen again?"

This he could answer. "We've set new initiatives in place, a more rigid system of checks and balances regarding who has access to funds, the number of people who are notified when a request for a withdrawal of funds is placed."

As the words came out, he heard the banality, the lack of individualism. A rote answer that contained important details. But one that failed to sell even him on the idea that the foundation wasn't at risk of making the same mistake twice.

What would he want to hear if he were being asked to invest in something? What would reassure him?

Bluntness. Honesty.

"It's not perfect. I want to say we will ensure something like this will never happen again. I can't promise that. But I can promise that we are doing everything in our power to reduce the likelihood of it happening. And I fully believe in the board of trustees and my current team to make

that happen, even as they understand and incor-
porate the additional oversight measures we've
put into place."

Ana slowly closed her notebook and threaded
her fingers together. Her eyes softened as she
smiled. "That was perfect, Shaw."

He arched a brow at her, trying not to let her see
how much the compliment affected him. "Even if
I didn't make a promise?"

"You made a real promise. That's worth more
than any perfectly crafted PR statement."

He leaned forward. "You've done this for a long
time, haven't you?"

The dark clouds gathering outside and the dim
glow of the dining car lights made it hard to dis-
cern details. But he could have sworn she paled
at his question.

"What do you mean?"

"Before coming to Edinburgh. You worked in
PR."

She slowly shook her head. "Not for a public
relations firm, no. But I volunteered a lot. Worked
with a hospital on fundraising, recruiting volun-
teers, that sort of thing."

"You were good at it."

Wistfulness touched her smile. "I was very
good at it. And I enjoyed it. I got to work with
the nurses and some of the hospital administra-
tors. But I also got to know a lot of the patients.
Hear their stories."

"Hence your preference for storytelling."

"Yes." She looked out the window again. Rain started to fall as the clouds pushed out the rest of the sunlight, making the landscape as dark as night. "I've met some amazing people and their families through the hospital. Ones who have agreed, or even volunteered, to have our committee share what they've been through. Numbers and statistics can go a long way, but the stories are what make the difference."

He wanted to tell her, he realized. Wanted to share why telling his story was so hard. Years of avoiding pain and eschewing connections made him stop. But what was the point in sharing? Of making himself vulnerable when nothing would come of it except more pain? There was no road out of this that left him intact. If he pursued anything romantic, he'd be breaching his own ethics. Even if he kept their relationship professional while sharing the hardest moments of his life and how much those events had influenced the foundation, Ana would be gone in three weeks, taking pieces of him with her he'd never intended to share. An act that almost seemed more intimate than a kiss.

The only logical road forward was to focus on the future and leave the past where it belonged.

"I think I'm going to head to my suite," Ana said as she stood. "I've been up late most nights working, and napping on a train in a thunderstorm sounds perfect."

"Of course." He followed suit and stood. "Sleep well." He waited until she was out of the car before he sat and scrubbed a hand over his face.

What was wrong with him? The more time he spent with Ana and saw the joy things like the scent of tea and the sight of a forgotten castle brought, the more he felt like he was emerging from a deep sleep, an existence that no longer seemed fulfilling. When he'd passed off the foundation's responsibilities to the board of trustees and a team of employees, he'd severed a bond. One that had kept him emotionally tied to something. Anything.

Was it the lack of emotional connections in his life that now made him respond so strongly to Ana? A susceptibility created by the stress of the past six months?

Or was it just Ana herself?

He shoved thoughts of Ana aside and pulled the shade down over the window. If he focused on his work, he could have a couple of productive hours before they arrived in London.

He kept his gaze on his computer and off the now empty seat across from him.

CHAPTER FOURTEEN

Shaw

SHAW STEPPED OFF the train and into the teeming rush of pedestrians streaming to and fro on the platforms of King's Cross Station. A ceiling of arched glass let in bright afternoon sunlight, a jarring change after the storm had followed them all the way to Peterborough. Languages rose and fell around him.

Past and present slammed together, melded. He saw himself sitting on a bench, watching as his mother tried to sell stems of wildflowers they'd picked along a roadside to get them back to Edinburgh. Saw the people hurrying past, faces turned away, collars turned up as they ignored the pleas of someone they labeled as just another beggar. Felt the scorching pain of his mother's embarrassment even as she squared her shoulders and did what needed to be done. To get them right back to where they had started with the bitter taste of fleeting happiness still lingering.

"Hey."

A hand rested on his shoulder, a comforting weight that yanked him out of the past. He looked down at Ana, saw the concern and compassion in her eyes. It wasn't hard to imagine her in a hospital, holding hands and offering words of comfort.

"You okay?"

"Yes." He gave her a small smile. "It's been a while since I've been here."

Just a couple years before his mother had died. Any time he'd come to London since then, he'd made sure to change trains so that he'd entered the city via a different station. Over time, it had become a habit. The painful memories of King's Cross had faded.

And now…now there was a sense of victory as they walked down the platform. Of not letting his past dictate his future. Of confronting it.

A taxi took them from the station to the Savoy. Shaw watched out of the corner of his eye as Ana took it all in, from the golden statue standing guard atop the canopy as they pulled up to the black-and-and-white-tiled lobby where they checked in.

"We're on the fifth floor," he said as they moved toward the elevators. "Two river-view suites."

As Ana pressed the button for the elevator, his phone rang.

"Shaw Harrington."

"Mr. Harrington." A smooth female voice with

a British accent greeted him. "Olivia Mahs. I trust your trip went smoothly?"

"It did." He paused, then added, "I was very impressed. Your chef's smoked salmon with cream sauce was exceptional."

"Thank you."

Olivia's voice warmed with genuine pleasure. Out of the corner of his eye, he saw Ana give him a thumbs-up.

"I apologize for the late notice, but would it be possible to move our meeting to tomorrow? I've been held up in Madrid."

Shaw frowned. His schedule had been planned to a *T* around this visit. But Olivia had been generous since the beginning of the Harrington Foundation, donating what had amounted to nearly three million pounds over the years.

"Of course. What time tomorrow?"

"Would one work?"

"Yes. Let's still plan on the Savoy, and I'll let you know if the location changes." Shaw hung up and turned to Ana. "Olivia's been held up until tomorrow. I understand if I need to send you back to Edinburgh."

The elevator doors opened, revealing a vivid green carpet trimmed in gold.

"No, I'm fine. It gives us another day to prepare." Ana glanced at her watch. "I had initially booked dinner at the Savoy Grill for tonight, but with your permission, I'll change the reservation to the hotel's afternoon tea tomorrow. I think that will appeal to someone like Olivia more."

The doors closed as she talked, verbalizing ideas and making little tweaks out loud as the elevator carried them up. Shaw listened, once again impressed with her knowledge and strategy.

"Then I need to work on the donor dinner plan." She glanced up at him as he grunted. "I want to be prepared to move on it if Olivia says yes. I'd prefer to have both her and Roy on board. But even if we have just one, I think it's still worth a shot."

"It is."

It was just the idea of making small talk with people while trying to sell them on reinvesting thousands of pounds into a foundation that had lost a significant chunk of their last donation that unsettled him.

Ana glance down, then back up at him. "When we get back, I could reach out to Kirstin and see if there's something I'm missing—"

"Don't." He turned to face her. "Don't question yourself. Just because I don't like the idea doesn't mean it's not a good one."

She looked down at her feet. "I don't want to fail."

"You mentioned that before."

A stray lock of hair rested against her face. He'd resisted touching her once. But he couldn't anymore, not after everything that had happened the past few days. He reached up and brushed it away, his fingertips grazing her cheek. Her head shot up, her sharp inhale echoing in the small space.

But she didn't pull away. No, she just continued to stare at him with those jewel-toned eyes as temptation smoldered between them.

"Who made you question yourself like this?"

She stared at him, eyes searching his face. Then her lips parted. The elevator dinged and the doors slid open.

Shaw dropped his hand. He should apologize. Should. But he couldn't bring himself to. That single touch, feeling the warmth of her skin, seeing the way she looked at him… He couldn't regret any of it.

"I'll get to work on that plan." Her voice sounded husky, breathless.

"I'm in the suite next to yours if you need anything."

She nodded before rushing down the hall and disappearing around the corner. He flexed his hand. Tried and failed to banish the memory of her gasp when he'd touched her.

Perhaps finding another location to work in, somewhere that wasn't in the room right next to hers, would be best. The change in his feelings over the last few days had left him drifting through his normally well-ordered existence, unable to grasp onto his usual control and keep himself in check. Just this morning he had resolved to keep his growing feelings to himself.

And here he was hours later brushing a stray curl off Ana's face.

He walked back into the elevator and pushed the button. Kirstin was coming back next week. It was probably the best possible thing to ensure that Shaw did not make a colossal mistake.

CHAPTER FIFTEEN

Eviana

EVIANA SCANNED OVER the draft of her event proposal. She'd rewritten it twice over the course of the afternoon. More, she suspected, out of the turmoil dancing at the edge of her mind than the plan needing much revision.

But it was good. Solid. A few phone calls had confirmed the restaurant she wanted was available. She'd emailed the plan to Kirstin, too, and was waiting to hear back. A productive afternoon.

Which was good because her morning had been anything but.

The train ride had started off well. But at some point she'd realized she was enjoying Shaw's company, not just professionally but personally. The surprise had been realizing he appeared to enjoy hers, too. Was she imagining the softening of his attitude? The lowering of his defenses? Was it all because of work? Or was he struggling, like she was, to keep things professional?

Nice didn't properly describe how wonderful it

was to be around someone and just…be. No pretenses, no false faces. Just be herself.

Guilt invaded, creeping through her contentment and filling her with a sense of shame. Eviana was being herself. But she was still lying to him.

She'd already been on edge when they'd arrived at the Savoy. And then Shaw had shocked her in the elevator by sliding that stray tendril of hair back. That graze of his fingers on her skin had been more intimate than any of the handful of kisses she'd experienced in her life. She'd nearly run to her room so she didn't do something stupid.

The tension between them was becoming a problem. No matter how much she told herself it wasn't, it reared its head again and again. Except this time she knew without a doubt Shaw felt it, too.

Unsure of what to say or how to handle the situation, she'd attempted to review her notes on Olivia Mahs and her history with the Harrington Foundation. When the words had clouded together and she'd realized she'd attempted to read the same paragraph five times, she'd thrown on a coat and gone for a walk.

The walk had been a much-needed refresher. The last time she had been in London had been years ago, when she'd traveled with her father and Nicholai to England for the late queen's Jubilee. They'd stayed at the Ritz in a royal suite with gilded trim and bodyguards stationed outside the doors at all hours. She'd been excited for the Jubilee and to meet the queen. But every time she'd asked if they could go somewhere, do something other than the rigorously scheduled list of royal events, she'd been told no, it wasn't a vacation but a duty. As they'd ridden through the procession past Buckingham Palace, she'd been so focused on keeping a smile on her face and waving as people shouted and snapped photos that the whole thing had passed by in a blur.

Walking past Buckingham Palace earlier had been peaceful. There'd been the usual tourists taking pictures, but none of the cameras had been aimed at her. Even with her blond hair and reading glasses on for extra measure, no one had glanced twice at a random tourist.

By the time she'd made it back to the hotel, her mind had quieted enough for her to focus on work. She'd spied Jodi only once, passing by the reading room downstairs where she had set up shop. Working in her room would have made her tense, listening for sounds from next door, wondering if Shaw was going to knock on her door and finally confront the friction between them.

So she'd chosen a plush chair in the ivory-colored room just off the main lobby and gotten to work, first on her review of Olivia and then polishing her proposal for a private dinner for twelve of Shaw's former donors.

Her computer let out a soft chime. Kirstin had emailed her back.

Love it! Excellent work. Small scale, which will appeal to Shaw, I'm sure, but still elegant enough to attract the donors. The handwritten invite from Shaw is a great touch. Hope he goes for it. If he doesn't, I'll see what I can do. Mum's doing great this week—be back on Monday!

Eviana smiled. Even from afar, Kirstin continued to be her cheerleader.

Her eyes rested on the last line.

…back on Monday!

Having Kirstin back would certainly change the dynamic between her and Shaw. For the better, she reminded herself. Although perhaps they just needed to have a conversation. Get everything out in the open. Acknowledge the attraction and then move forward.

"Ana."

Eviana's head jerked up. Shaw was casually leaning against the black door frame.

"Oh. Hi."

Even though she hadn't said her thoughts out loud, it didn't stop the heat from climbing up her throat and into her cheeks.

"How was your afternoon?" he asked.

"Good." She cleared her throat. "Yours?"

"Productive." He moved into the room, eyes sweeping over the raised paneling on the walls, the plush emerald couch she'd claimed, the vase of elegant red roses behind her. "Cozy spot."

"Yes."

He looked at her then, that familiar intensity back again. "Why didn't you work in your room?"

She started to come up with an answer, something appropriate. And then decided to do exactly what Shaw had encouraged her to do and speak her mind.

"I wasn't sure how things stood between us after the elevator. I decided to keep my distance until I could figure out how to approach it."

He sat down in the chair across from her as she closed her computer. Then he gave her that slight smile she had come to enjoy so much. "I did, too."

"What?"

"Worked somewhere else."

She stared at him for a moment before sitting back and letting out a frustrated laugh. "We're a pair."

"Yes." He leaned forward, folding his arms as his face hardened. "Did I make you uncomfortable?"

"No! I mean…" The heat in her cheeks deepened. "No. Not uncomfortable. It's just…" She blew out a breath. "I find you very attractive."

His mouth curved up into a slight smirk. "Thank you."

"Working with you like this, so closely…" Her voice trailed off, and she ran a hand through her hair. "It's made it harder to ignore."

"I know. It has been for me, too."

The pressure on her lungs eased. "Good. Not that you had to ignore anything. Just… I'm glad it wasn't just me."

His blue eyes warmed a fraction. "It's not just you."

For a moment they stared at each other, endless possibilities drifting between them.

And then he sat back. "But we both know nothing can come of this."

She nodded, focusing on her sense of relief that they were on the same page instead of the hard ball of disappointment settling in her stomach. "You're effectively my boss. And I'm going home."

He started to say something, then stopped.

"What?" she asked.

"Nothing. I have no right to ask."

"Shaw, please," she said. "If we're clearing the air, we might as well as get everything out in the open."

"Is there anyone else?"

His words made her pulse pound faster.

"No. It's been a long time since I've been on a date."

"Me, too."

A different kind of relief coursed through her. *Even though it doesn't make a difference.*

"I want to keep this professional for myself, my work ethic, and for Kirstin. She's done so much in such a short time," Eviana said. "I don't want to get involved with a client and have that come back on her down the road."

"Understood. I refuse to get romantically involved with an employee."

Silence fell between them. Soft conversations and the lilting notes of piano music drifted in from the lobby.

"So…what now?" Eviana finally asked. "Do we just keep our distance?"

"No," he said. "We go back to how things were without the underlying tension."

It sounded simple enough. And she felt more at ease with him than she had in…well, ever since they'd met. The attraction was still there. But now that it had been acknowledged with a mutual agreement that they wouldn't act on it, the tension had disappeared.

"I think I'd like that," she said.

"Good." He stood. "Because I'd hate to eat alone for dinner."

She grinned. "You seem exactly like the kind of person who would love to eat alone."

"Once in a while, even stuffy, private millionaires like company."

This was better. Much better. They could have dinner like civilized adults, converse, work together. And, she told herself as she followed Shaw to the elevators, over time, the attraction would fade. She would return to Kelna. Eventually she would find someone, fall in love, get married. The memory of her brief time with Shaw would be a pleasant one, something to return to and reminisce about on hard days.

It would be enough.

CHAPTER SIXTEEN

Shaw

ANA'S EYES WIDENED as they walked into the Beaufort Bar. "It's like stepping back into the roaring twenties."

Her eyes devoured everything, from the signature burnt-orange chairs with curved backs to the black walls decorated with strategically placed mirrors. Coupled with the soft lighting, the overall atmosphere was reminiscent of a glamorous speakeasy.

"Compared to the history of the Savoy itself," he said as he nodded to the maître d' he'd spoken with on his way down to the reading room, "a relatively new addition."

"It's incredible. This has to be the nicest bar I've ever been in."

"Do you go to bars often?" he asked with a slight chuckle as they were seated at a table for two in a corner of the room.

She laughed. "Actually, the first time I was ever

in a bar was two months ago when I arrived in Edinburgh."

Shaw frowned. "You hadn't been inside a bar before?"

"No, my father didn't…" She stopped. Her eyes dropped to the table, then back up to his. "Image was very important to my father. And he had good reason," she added. "He had a certain esteem in our community. His image was a part of the work he did. I was a reflection of that."

Anger stirred deep in his gut. "That's a lot to place on a child."

"It was." The smile she gave him was sad but accepting. "It's hard to explain. It's not something I enjoyed. But it was a necessity."

"I flinch at the thought of a dinner with a dozen people. I can't fathom having to always be on alert."

The sadness in her eyes deepened. Just for a moment, but so heart-wrenching it made him want to reach out and touch her again, offer something that would chase the sorrow from her face.

Then it was gone as she broke eye contact and picked up the menu. "These drinks look incredible."

He wanted to pursue the topic, ask more questions and learn about the history she so carefully hid. But he also wanted to make the evening a happy one.

"What was your first drink?" he asked as he picked up his own menu.

"A beer."

"Was it any good?"

"Terrible," Ana said with another laugh. "I found a couple I've liked since then. But I definitely prefer wine and cocktails."

"Then you're not going to be disappointed tonight."

They ordered drinks. He went outside his usual parameters and ordered a whisky cocktail. She ordered a gin drink mixed with sparkling wine and violet syrup, topped off with a purple flower perched perfectly on the edge of the glass. They dined on grilled prawns, sourdough smothered in toasted cheese, and plump red grapes.

"May I ask you a personal question?"

Shaw looked up from the chocolate mousse they'd ordered for dessert. "Yes. I may not answer it, but you can always ask me anything."

She gave him a small smile. "Fair. You mentioned you hadn't been to King's Cross Station in a long time. You looked...sad."

He set his fork down and picked up his drink. When she continued to stare at him, he quirked an eyebrow. "I didn't hear the question."

She rolled her eyes even as her lips tilted up. "What happened?"

Shaw took a sip of his cocktail, the smooth flavor of whisky melding perfectly with the sweetness of orange and ruby port. For the past few days, he'd wanted to know Ana more. To have her share a piece of herself. Yet he had done nothing to earn that trust. Had shared almost nothing of himself other than a couple of hints and a photograph.

"My father deserted my mother when I was two years old. I don't really have any memories of him. Just her."

The light in Ana's eyes dimmed. "I'm sorry."

"Don't be. From what little my mother said, he was interested in her until I came along. They made it work for a couple years, but one day he just decided he didn't want to be a father. So he left."

Ana's mouth twisted into a scowl. "Dobber."

He smiled. Truly smiled for the first time in he couldn't remember how long. "Precisely." He used the stir stick in his glass to move the candied orange peel around, watching it dance among the amber liquid. "They weren't well off, but he had told her to stay home with me. When he left, she had nothing. She was injured a year later when she was crossing the street on her way to a job as a maid at a hotel. Her leg was never the same, and it became difficult for her to work. We lived in Edinburgh for years." He focused his attention on the bar, watched a bartender pour contents into a silver shaker. "When I was twelve, we came to London. There was a charity here that promised to get her set up with work, a place to live. And they did. We had two good years."

The best years. Years when his mother had gone to work as a receptionist for a doctor. When they had splurged on slices of carrot and hazelnut cake at Borough Market or visited the zoo every month. When his mother had laughed instead of cried herself to sleep when she'd thought he couldn't hear her.

"What happened?" Ana gently prompted.

His hands tightened around the glass. His fury at Zach and what he'd done was nothing compared to the rage that had consumed him all those years ago. Days after his fourteenth birthday, when the life he and his mother had come to know had been ripped away from them by someone else's greed.

"The charity that helped us with housing lost their funding."

A hand settled on top of his. Shaw stilled. Then, slowly, he turned his head and looked at Ana. There was no pity. No judgment or disgust. There was just Ana. Compassionate, kind, supportive. Grieving for a woman she'd never met and the boy he had been.

He breathed in. "We made it for a month or two. But without rent support, we had to move out of the apartment. It was too expensive to stay in London, so Mam and I came back to Edinburgh." His jaw tightened. "We took a train from King's Cross. We picked wildflowers along the way and tried to sell them in the station to earn some extra money. People…they weren't cruel, but they weren't kind, either. Just…indifferent."

Her fingers tightened over his. "Indifference can be its own kind of cruelty."

"Yes. Like we weren't even worth acknowledging."

Ana squeezed his hand once more before sitting back. He felt the loss of her touch as he curled his fingers into his palm.

"Thank you. For sharing with me."

Her voice was husky, raw, as if she were holding back tears. That his confession had meant something to her made it worth it. Even if it had left him feeling exposed. Unmasked.

"I've never told anyone that."

Her shoulders rose up a fraction and she looked away. Uneasiness curled in his stomach.

"What?"

"I just…" She shook her head. "You told me something so personal. And I… I feel like I can't…"

"I won't betray anything you tell me, Ana. But it's your story to tell. And you did tell me something," he reminded her. "Your first time in a bar."

Her shoulders relaxed as she chuckled. "True."

"What else do you want to do?"

She gave him a quizzical look. "What?"

"What else haven't you done that you want to?"

The shy smile she gave him pierced his chest

and lodged in the vicinity of his heart. "Have you ever been up in the London Eye?"

"The giant Ferris wheel? No."

"Me neither. I was only in London once before and didn't get to do much. Maybe I'll stay in London for a few days on my way home."

Impulse seized him. He pulled out his phone and pulled up the website. "You're in luck. The last rotation will start in forty minutes. We can make it if we leave now."

He held up his phone. The smile she gave him when she saw the e-tickets on the screen made him feel like he had just conquered a mountain peak.

After telling the waiter to bill the meal to his room, they hurried out of the bar and down to the main floor. A quick conversation with the concierge had a taxi ready and waiting for them as they walked out. Ana kept her eyes glued to the window as they passed the fountains of Trafalgar Square, the imposing facade of Whitehall and the timeless silhouette of Big Ben against the darkening sky.

As the taxi sped across Westminster Bridge, Ana tore her gaze away from the scenery and smiled at him. "Thank you, Shaw."

What he had said to her in the reading room, his promise to maintain his distance, now hung like a chain around his neck. He'd never before doubted his ability to stay indifferent, to keep himself re-moved from those around him.

Yet the woman next to him had him question-ing everything.

The taxi pulled up to the curb. Ana started to pull out her wallet.

"Not a chance."

She narrowed her eyes at him. "You paid for dinner and for the tickets. The least I can do is spring for a taxi."

He swiped his card in the machine behind the driver's seat. Ana started to protest, but he slid out of the cab and held out his hand. She reluctantly accepted it, grumbling as he closed the door be-hind her.

"We're going to miss our ride if we stand here arguing," he said.

"I'm not arguing," she retorted as they moved down the sidewalk. "I just don't want you to think I expect you to pay for everything."

"The fact that you don't makes me want to."

She let out a confused laugh. "What?"

"I enjoy giving a gift to someone who appre-ciates it." He glanced down at her as they neared the ticket booth. "I want to do this for you, Ana."

Her steps slowed as confusion clouded her face. "Shaw—"

"Please."

She let out a small laugh. "How can I refuse?"

"I'm sold out of tickets," the attendant said as they approached.

Shaw held up his phone. "I believe I bought the last one."

"Oh." The attendant glanced at her watch, then smiled at them. "Perfect timing."

Ana's smile stretched from ear to ear as they walked up the queue. The wheel rotated continuously, so slow it was easy to step off the boarding platform and into the capsule. A giant bubble with a long bench in the middle and huge glass windows that provided 360-degree views of London.

"This is beautiful," Ana breathed.

Shaw's chest tightened. What would it be like to take joy in so many things, big and small?

As the wheel rotated higher, he tried. Tried to let go of the usual facts and figures he thought of and focus on his surroundings. A boat gliding across the water on the river below. The face of Big Ben glowed against a violet-colored sky.

Tension he didn't even realize he'd been carrying eased as he watched the world around him.

"When I go back home," Ana said softly, "I'll be taking on a much larger role in my family's organization."

Shaw stayed where he was, partly out of respect but also because a greedy part of him didn't want to spook her.

"I've always known I would be involved in it. But my father..." Her voice caught. She wrapped her arms around herself. "Logically, I know there's an end. But I always thought…"

He moved then, going to her side and wrapping an arm around her shoulders. He had never been swayed by physical touch. But the need to touch Ana was a living, breathing need inside of him.

"I thought the same of my mother."

She leaned into him. "We knew for some time that we were going to lose him. It gave us some time to prepare. But the weight of everything fell on my brother. He was going to be so wrapped up in it all that he was going to lose out on the chance to be with someone he really loved."

"Not to play devil's advocate, but wasn't that his choice? To choose work over his personal life?"

Ana shook her head. "It's…it's hard to explain."

That was what she had said about her father's expectations of her. What did her family do that would warrant such pressure?

"I understood why he was at the crossroads he was. So I offered to step up and take on a larger role."

His arm tightened about her shoulders. "Is it something you want to do?"

"Yes and no. I liked what I did before. This… it comes with so much more responsibility and expectations."

"To be someone you're not."

She looked up at him then, eyes wide and glimmering green beneath the soft lighting of the car.

"That's what it feels like. Just before I came to Edinburgh, I made a mistake. One that made me question whether I'm right for the role."

"So don't do it."

The smile she gave him was bleak, almost hopeless. "It's not that simple."

"Why not? What is it that your family does?"

A shutter dropped over her face. She started to pull away, but he gripped her shoulders and turned her to face him.

"I didn't mean to pry. I just...you deserve more than that."

Slowly, one hand came up and rested on his. "Thank you. I know I sound hypocritical, telling you to share more when I tell you almost nothing about myself."

"One, you don't owe me anything, Ana. Ever," he said emphatically. "I want to know more about you, yes. But it's your choice, and yours alone, as to what you do and do not share with me."

Her brows drew together. "I appreciate that, but I've been pushing you to—"

"To share necessary information to get the donors who supported a charitable foundation a reason to trust me again."

As he said the words out loud, something slid into place, an understanding of what Ana had been trying to achieve. Logically, he'd heard her words, read her proposal. But now he understood the why.

"Never once have you pushed me to share my life with you. Even when I told you what I did about my childhood, you didn't press. You listened. You supported." He stepped closer as he moved one hand to cup her cheek. "Stop being so hard on yourself."

Her lips parted. His thumb drifted over her cheek, rubbing gentle, soothing circles across her skin. The air in the car changed, became charged with the tension they had both sworn to dismiss yet couldn't keep at bay.

Shaw stared down into Ana's eyes. Saw his own yearning reflected back to him.

Tomorrow he would make amends. But tonight...

He leaned down, savored her sharp inhale, the sight of her lashes drifting down as she closed her eyes.

And then he kissed her.

Eviana

The gentle pressure of Shaw's lips on hers filled Eviana with a warmth she hadn't even imagined possible. One that made her feel beautiful, cherished, wanted.

She rose up, pressing her body against him as she wrapped her arms around his neck. A groan sounded against her lips a moment before Shaw banded an arm around her waist and pulled her even closer, as if he didn't want to leave even a sliver of light between them.

Slowly, tentatively, she slid one hand up the back of his neck, her fingers delving into his hair. The feel of his silky hair contrasted with the hardness of his body against hers, sending a delicious shiver of sensation through her.

Joy filled her. Pure, unadulterated joy. She moaned softly, then smiled against his mouth as he angled his head and took her deeper.

She had been kissed before. But never like this. Never by someone she felt so connected to, who wanted to know the real her.

Except he doesn't.

The thought slammed into her, filling her veins with ice as her stomach dropped to her feet. She pulled back.

"Shaw…" She shook her head, trying to keep her tears at bay. "I… I can't."

He held her against him for another long moment, confusion and frustration evident in the lines of his face, the hardness in his eyes.

But he released her and stepped back.

"I'm leaving in three weeks. And this," she said as she gestured between them, "this isn't just some fling. This is…"

Embarrassed, she moved back to the windows. All of London was spread out before her, from the towering walls of Buckingham Palace to the dome of St. Paul's Cathedral. One of the most incredible views in England, and all she could think of was the man behind her. The man she was finally coming to accept would sneak past any defenses she erected simply by being himself.

"I know." She sensed him behind her, swore she could feel the warmth from his body at her back even though he didn't touch her. "It's the same for me."

She choked back a sob. In another life, they might have had something. If her father hadn't gotten ill, if she didn't have a life of duty waiting for her back home, if…

Too many ifs. None of them mattered. This was now, and nothing could change the trajectory she was on. Even if Shaw did accept who she was, their paths in life would never mesh. Her entire life would revolve around the kind of things Shaw hated. She had taken this sabbatical because she had struggled with the demands on her time and on her person. She couldn't, wouldn't, ask someone else to join her, especially someone like Shaw, knowing her role would slowly eat away at him.

But that didn't stop how she felt about him. How much her feelings had deepened in just a couple days.

The wheel continued to rotate, slowly taking the car back toward the ground. They stood in silence and watched London go by. She could see his reflection in the glass, the hard line in his jaw juxtaposed against the kaleidoscope of emotions in his eyes.

He'd given her so much tonight. Except she had been the one to pull back, to push him away.

Eviana vowed in that moment to tell Shaw the truth. Not now, when her heart was bruised and bleeding. But just before she left. She would tell him everything, including how much she was coming to care for him. He might be angry or disappointed. But at least she would tell him, and maybe one day, he would understand why she'd had to leave.

CHAPTER SEVENTEEN

Shaw

A LILTING MELODY drifted from the piano in the center of the Thames Foyer, a glass-domed atrium that hosted afternoon tea at the Savoy. China cups clinked as people conversed quietly, the occasional laugh sounding through the room. Tiered trays were delivered to tables with artfully arranged bites like artichoke tarts and blueberry scones, as well as plates filled with sandwiches like chicken, pickled cucumber and smoked salmon. An elegant afternoon spent at one of London's oldest hotels.

An environment Eviana had insisted would appeal to a woman like Olivia Mahs.

The woman in question sat across from Shaw, her gaze sweeping around the room. Tall with short, curly hair and round glasses, she exuded confidence and class.

Shaw kept his gaze focused on Olivia and off of Ana. A nearly impossible feat, given how incredible she looked today.

Focus, Shaw.

The rest of their ride on the Eye and subsequent taxi trip back to the hotel had been silent. As if they had finally tasted what could be yet knew nothing more could happen. They'd texted briefly that morning. But the first time he had seen her since bidding her good-night in the lobby had been when he had walked out of the elevator and found Ana conversing with Olivia.

For a moment, he hadn't been able to tear his eyes away. In her red trousers, black silk top and white blazer, she had looked more confident and more self-assured than he had ever seen her. With her hair pulled up into a bun high on top of her head, the unique angles and planes of her face had been on full display.

He'd allowed himself one moment, just one, to drink in the sight of her. To savor the pride at seeing her wear bright colors once more instead of the bland black-and-white ensembles that had never seemed like her.

Like Ana. Bold, beautiful, kind.

And then he'd slipped back into his old armor as he'd mentally prepared for the battle in front of him.

"I'm curious, Mr. Harrington," Olivia said now as she raised her glass to her lips, "what you think you have to say that could persuade me to resume my donations to the Harrington Foundation given that nearly one hundred percent of my contributions from last year were lost to an investment

fraud perpetrated by a man you personally nom-
inated to be CEO."

Straight to the jugular, then.

"A valid question, Miss Mahs. But before I answer, I'd like to apologize."

Olivia blinked in surprise. "For?"

"Even though my role with the foundation is
primarily ceremonial at this point, I created it.
And you're right—I recommended Zach for the
position because he had many of the qualities I
lack."

Out of the corner of his eye, he saw Ana look
down. For one moment, he wondered if he had
screwed up. But then he saw the slightest upward
tilt of her lips, felt her approval.

He took the strength she silently offered and
continued. "I also did it because I wanted someone else to be the face. Had I not taken the easy
way out and been more involved, this might not
have happened."

Olivia regarded him over the rim of her glass
for a long moment. "Perhaps." She plucked a brioche bun off the tiered tray. "But men like Zachary White know just what to say. I should know,"
she said wryly. "He made quite the impression
on me when we met in New York five years ago.
Obviously, given that I became a recurring donor
that same night."

"He was persuasive. But," Shaw continued, "I
also had some concerns. Ones I pushed to the side

because I didn't want to do the hard work or put myself out there."

Silence descended. Olivia watched him over the rim of her glass as she took a long sip of her rosé. As if baiting him to say something more, to see how long he could last while she evaluated him.

"May I add something, Mr. Harrington?"

He looked at Ana. She gazed back at him, a neutral expression and that subtle smile on her face. But her eyes…her eyes glinted with determination, conviction.

"Yes, Miss Barros. Please."

Ana turned to Olivia. "I've only been working with Mr. Harrington for a couple weeks. But in that time, I've come to see how much he cares about the foundation and the people it serves. When he says he didn't want to do the hard work, I have to disagree. He made a mistake that many have. You yourself stated you were swayed by Zachary. That Mr. Harrington was fooled, too, should not be held against him."

He blinked at the daring of her words. Whether Olivia Mahs would accept Ana's reasoning was one thing. But it didn't stop the pride that filled him at Ana speaking with this combination of professionalism and courage.

"That he's here now," Ana continued, "is a testament to how much he cares about the foundation and how much he personally wants to make things right."

Olivia regarded her thoughtfully. "Noted." She smiled at Ana before refocusing on Shaw. "Proceed, Mr. Harrington."

Shaw launched into the pitch he and Ana had worked on. An international hiring process for a new CEO. New additions to the accounting department that would implement a series of checks and balances. Creating a public relations department to support the already strained marketing team and help better share the stories of the charities and people they helped.

"Even as our financial capabilities have plummeted," he said, "we've managed to sustain all of our charities in some capacity, with our board of trustees helping identify the ones who need the most urgent funding."

Olivia tilted her head to the side. "How have you been able to maintain your operations to that degree?"

Shaw glanced at Ana, who slightly shook her head. She hadn't said anything to Olivia about his contributions. But sometimes achieving something monumental demanded sacrifice.

"I have been making routine investments in the foundation since the crisis."

Olivia's gaze sharpened. "How much?"

"Three million."

She stared at him for so long, assessing, that he resigned himself to the inevitable. He hadn't done his job. Hadn't sold her on—

"All right."

He blinked. "Excuse me?"

"I'll resume my donations."

A slow exhale escaped as relief surged through him. "Thank you, Miss Mahs."

"Olivia." She smiled at him. "I admire and respect someone who believes in something enough he'll put his own money into it. Especially to right a wrong, even if he's not the one who perpetrated it."

"Your support will mean a great deal to the organizations we support."

She inclined her head. "That does come with the stipulation that if at any time I feel uncomfortable, I will cancel my donations."

"Of course."

"Miss Mahs," Ana said, "I know we've already asked a great deal of you, but—"

"Olivia," the older woman insisted with a gentle smile. "But?"

Ana launched into an overview of the dinner. Shaw watched as she rattled off the guest list, explaining the need for Olivia's support, drawing the event back to the need for reestablishing the foundation to meet the needs in the United Kingdom. The passion in her voice, the genuineness as she spoke about a specific organization that offered pediatric and maternal healthcare in rural communities the Scottish Highlands, drew him in as if he was hearing about his own foundation for the first time.

"Yes."

Olivia's voice yanked him out of his reverie.

Ana's lips parted. "Yes?"

"Yes," Olivia repeated. "I wasn't comfortable with canceling my donations to the foundation. But given that I had just been given the assignment of overseeing the final rollout of my family's railroad to the public, I was concerned that my choices would be under additional scrutiny." A frown darkened her face. "Personal reasons I should have thought about more before making such a drastic decision."

Shaw hesitated, then took a leap. "My mother and I relied on the services of a charity when I was younger. The CEO of the charity embezzled funds to purchase a house and travel. We lost everything because of it, as did a number of others."

He heard Ana's gasp. But he didn't look at her. Couldn't. Not when he had just revealed something so monumental.

"I'm sorry," Olivia said softly. "I had no idea."

"It was that experience that led me to create the Harrington Foundation. That and my mother." His chest tightened. "She persevered through some very hard times. When Zach told me what he'd done, I felt betrayed. A betrayal I'm sure you and our other donors felt, too."

"I already felt confident in my decision." Olivia lifted her teacup in a toast. "But now I'm certain of it."

Eviana

Eviana sat in the dining car, her notes on the dinner spread out before her. The meeting with Olivia had been an unprecedented success. Olivia had stayed for another thirty minutes, guiding the conversation to their experience on the train trip to London and asking for feedback on what could be improved. It had proven to be a very enjoyable afternoon.

Satisfaction bubbled in her chest. She'd done it—balanced speaking her mind with the professional calm Helena was always encouraging. It had been easy to be confident with Kirstin, to think she was improving while cocooned in the safe environment of Murray PR's office. But going out on a limb, with Shaw's encouragement, had been a test. One she'd forced herself to take on and passed.

She glanced out the window as houses gave way to pastures. Night turned the grass dark as stars winked into existence overhead. In just a few hours, she and Shaw would be back in Edinburgh. Returning to a completely different dynamic given what had transpired between them in London.

Whether it had been the exhilaration from their achievement or relief at finally having some good news, she and Shaw had managed to maintain a pleasant, albeit stilted, conversation on the taxi ride to the train station.

Now, as he sat across from her, fingers flying across his keyboard, she couldn't help but glance at his handsome profile. His sudden confession had rocked her. Learning last night of the struggles he and his mother had faced, followed by the betrayal they had experienced at the hands of someone who had promised to care for them, had left her speechless.

Even on her hardest days, she had never experienced such heartbreak. Which only made her respect him more. Respect and...

She swallowed hard. Feelings that went far deeper than she was prepared to deal with. Their kiss last night had left her wanting. Yes, she wanted to explore their physical attraction, but she also longed for something more. For the first time, she had tasted true desire: the need for a man who had accepted her, and wanted her, for who she was.

For who he thought she was.

Heat pricked her eyes. Not only was she still lying to Shaw about her identity, there was no future for them. Shaw's life was here, in Edinburgh. Or in New York, depending on what he decided to do. Regardless, it did not include a life with a princess. A life that would demand so much.

Too much.

"I'm going to go back to my suite."

Shaw glanced up at her and frowned. "Are you feeling all right?"

"Just tired," she said. "Like I ran a marathon."

His slight smile nearly undid her. "We essentially did." He glanced at his watch. "Two hours before we get to Edinburgh. I've arranged to have a car take you to your apartment."

This time Eviana didn't even feel irritated that he had arranged things. She was just grateful. Especially because she knew the coming days would demand more of her. The days between now and the dinner would be filled to the brim. Plenty to stay focused on and keep her mind off that amazing kiss.

"Thank you. I…"

There was so much she wanted to say. How she admired everything he had overcome. How deeply she respected him for putting himself out on a limb for what he believed in. How much she appreciated the trust he had placed in her. All professional feelings.

But it was the emotions that ran deeper, that were very much not professional, that held her tongue.

"See you in a bit," she said.

She walked out of the dining room and moved quickly from train car to train car until she reached her suite. Eviana darted inside and closed the door behind her, locking it with a quick twist before buying her face in her hands.

She'd known for some time it wasn't just a simple crush. But this...this awareness of him whenever he was in the room, the joy she had experienced on their dash across London and the first part of their trip up in the Eye, the ease of just being around him...

A knock sounded on her door.

She frowned. "Who is it?"

"Shaw."

His voice sounded through the door, deep and raw. She felt the need in his voice, closed her eyes as she stood on a mental precipice.

And then she unlocked the door.

Shaw filled the doorway, his breathing ragged, his eyes burning.

Did he move first? Did she?

Does it matter? she thought desperately as they crashed into each other.

His lips captured hers. She wound her arms around his neck, moaned as his hands pressed against her back and urged her closer.

It was as if they both knew this would be their last time. Their last kiss before they returned to Edinburgh, to real life. Here, on this train speeding through the twilight landscape, they had a few precious moments. Ones they greedily took as the kiss deepened, hearts pounding in tandem.

She should have pulled him into her suite. Kissing him in the doorway, when anyone could walk down the hallway, was risky.

But the greater risk would be inviting him in and closing the door behind him. So instead, for this one moment, she would throw caution to the wind and savor her stolen kisses.

Shaw slid a hand up her neck, his fingers giving one deft yank that sent her hair spilling over her shoulders.

"So beautiful, Ana."

She froze.

Eviana. My name is Eviana.

"Shaw…" She pulled back but selfishly kept her arms around his neck as she buried her face in his chest and breathed in his scent. "I…"

"I know." His touch gentled, his hand stroking over her hair.

"I want to ask you in."

"It's wrong."

She choked back a sob. He was speaking to his role as her boss. But he didn't know, couldn't know what was truly holding her back. The lie between them that had seemed so inconsequential in the beginning but now loomed like a phantom just outside her door.

"I want to come in," he murmured against her hair.

"I know." She squeezed her eyes shut. "I know you can't."

They stood there in the doorway, breaths mingling, hearts thudding, grief and longing filling the air.

He leaned down. His lips grazed her temple.

And then he slowly released her before he walked away, leaving her alone in the doorway. She watched as he stopped outside his door and slid a key into the lock.

He stopped, one hand on the key, his head turned slightly.

A tear slid down her cheek as she closed the door to her room and locked it.

CHAPTER EIGHTEEN

Eviana
Two weeks later

THE SECRET GARDEN room of the famed Witchery boutique hotel and restaurant lived up to both its name and reputation. Huge arched doors dominated one wall and provided a tantalizing glimpse of the patio. Dark stone and wood created an atmosphere of intimacy, enhanced by the candles flickering on the tables.

Private. Elegant. One of Edinburgh's culinary treasures.

Perfect.

Eviana circled the room for the fourth time, eyes sweeping over the table settings, the flowers. A table had been set up on the other side of the room with photos from some of the charities supported by the Harrington Foundation, along with letters from grateful clients, case managers and boards.

It had been her idea, one she hadn't been sure Shaw would like. But he'd agreed to it. In fact, he'd agreed to almost everything since they'd returned from London.

Her gaze darted to the stairs, then back to the room. Every meeting since their train ride had included Kirstin. By mutual unspoken agreement, they'd refrained from any situation where they might be alone. Instead, they'd both knuckled down—she and Kirstin with the upcoming dinner and public relations evaluation, and Shaw with the restructuring of the Harrington Foundation.

Eviana wandered over to the table with the pictures and letters. Her fingers drifted across a letter written in crayon. The child had written to thank the Harrington Foundation for helping find his father a job. He'd drawn a stick figure of his father pushing a lawnmower at his new job as a groundskeeper.

So many people. So many that had been given a supporting hand from a man who knew the value of helping others. A man who knew the pain of being left to flounder.

She turned away from the table. Shaw hadn't said any more about his experiences in London. Every now and then, she thought of his mother's photograph, wondered what happened between their return to Edinburgh and his mother's passing. What Shaw had gone through as he'd fought his way from poverty to the top of the financial world.

.But it was none of her concern. Even after she

finally shared with him who she was, he would owe her nothing. No more stories of his own past unless he wanted to share. At this point, she just hoped he would still talk to her after finding out she was a princess living incognito.

No matter what, she reminded herself as she adjusted a stack of brochures she'd worked on with the marketing department, she was going home stronger. Working with someone who had encouraged her to be herself, coupled with the success of their meeting with Olivia, had been nearly as freeing as coming to Edinburgh.

The doubts still circled. They probably would until she returned home. But they didn't rule her waking thoughts. When she thought of her snafu of a speech, she could think about it critically, analyze what had gone wrong and what she would do differently in the future.

Starting with writing her own speeches. Input from Helena and her team was fine. But if she was going to be a leader, she'd start by being the leader she realized she could be, not a puppet tailored to follow protocol.

As she walked across the dining room, awareness pricked between her shoulder blades. She knew even before she turned that Shaw would be walking down the stairs.

She faced him, giving him a polite smile even though the only other person in the room was a waiter lighting the last remaining candles. Shaw's eyes swept over her, warming with appreciation as he took in her dress. Pale blue, with one shoulder left bare and the other featuring a long length of wispy material trailing down her back, it made her feel elegant and just a touch daring.

"You look beautiful."

"Thank you." Hoping he didn't notice the tremble in her voice, she gestured to his dark blue tuxedo. "The tie was the right choice."

His smile set off a flurry of butterflies in her stomach. Despite the lingering tension between them, he had smiled so much more in the past two weeks. Enough that Kirstin had commented on it a couple days ago.

Maybe he has a girlfriend, Kirstin had said jokingly.

The thought of Shaw dating had left Eviana sick to her stomach.

"I certainly prefer this to the bow tie." He tugged on the end and slightly dislodged the knot.

"Oh." Without thinking, she moved forward and started to undo the tie before she realized what she was doing. "I'm sorry!" She started to step back. "I just… I do this—"

"It's fine." The huskiness in his voice slid over her, under her skin, leaving little trails of want behind. "It sounds like some guests are already here, so if you wouldn't mind…"

She focused on the material, trying to move quickly while tying with precision.

"You said you do this often?"

She smiled slightly. "For my brother. At least I used to. He'd get nervous before…" She stopped, swallowed her words. "His fiancée does it for him now."

Silence settled between them. She could feel his disappointment, his withdrawal as she finished tying.

So many secrets between them.

"Thank you, Miss Barros."

His words cut through her like a knife. But she was the one who had kept this barrier between them, who hadn't trusted him with her identity.

He stepped back, started to turn away. After tonight, she had one week left. One week before she returned to Kelna and most likely never saw Shaw Harrington again.

"Shaw."

His head snapped around. "Yes?"

She swallowed hard. "Tonight…after the dinner, could I…"

Voices filtered in from above. Shaw glanced toward the stairs, his shoulders going rigid.

"Sorry, what?"

"It can wait." She breathed in, resumed her mantle of professionalism as people began descending the stairs. "There's something I'd like to share with you tonight before you go."

He gave her a vague nod as he moved to the base of the stairs to greet the first couple. Eviana let out a harsh breath. She'd taken the first step. If everything went well tonight, she'd tell him. If it didn't…she would reassess then.

But it will go well.

She couldn't believe, after all the hard work everyone had put in, that at least some of the donors wouldn't agree to come back. She snagged a glass of champagne from a passing waiter.

Showtime.

The event kicked off with a cocktail hour. Kirstin, Eviana, Shaw and members of the board circulated among the guests. Shaw conversed and even occasionally laughed as he spoke with each donor. Pride filled Eviana's chest as he greeted people by name, shook their hands and remembered details like new grandbabies being born and recent graduations. Details that surprised his guests and left more than one watching Shaw with curiosity and appreciation. Even Roy and Victoria Miles had joined, although Roy had been unusually subdued.

Waiters served venison, barbecued halibut and grilled jackfruit for the vegetarians in attendance, alongside tomatoes dusted with grated pistachios, baked asparagus drizzled with hollandaise and burrata mixed with a garlic pesto and served on toasted brioche. Eviana dined with a banker from Switzerland and her husband. Besotted with their first grandbaby who had just turned one, Eviana was treated to numerous stories and a carousel of pictures featuring the lovely little girl in various stages of smashing a cake.

At one point, she looked up and saw Shaw watching her. He returned her small nod before turning back to his dinner companions. A museum curator from Spain and her sister, Eviana remembered. Watching both women converse, and the younger one subtly flirt, with Shaw tested her ability to focus. But she pushed through, keeping her eyes off his table as much as possible and on her dinner companions.

After the dinner plates had been cleared away and waiters brought in an array of desserts, from Scottish oatcake served with ginger chutney to chocolate torte topped with pear ice cream, Shaw stood. Conversations gradually died off as everyone turned their attention to him.

Eviana sat back in her chair, hands folded, pulse pounding as he glanced around the room.

"I hope everyone enjoyed their meal." He smiled as a murmur of approval swept through the room. "I'm glad. When I was a boy, I would walk by the gate for this restaurant. I'd see the people going in, never imagining that one day I would be one of them."

Eviana's heartbeat kicked up a notch as people exchanged confused glances with one another.

"Most of you don't know, but I grew up in Edinburgh. My mother and I occasionally had a roof over our heads. But there were plenty of times when we stayed in shelters or, one particularly hard time, in a car."

The room fell silent, save for the occasional crackle of a candle.

"I've never shared my history with anyone until just recently." He looked at Eviana again. Emotion flared in his eyes. Just for a second, but long enough to steal the breath from her lungs. "I know the Harrington Foundation has lost your trust. Why would you invest your money into an organization that just lost millions?

"I'm speaking to you tonight not as the founder, but as a man who for two years benefitted from the generosity of a charity in London. One that provided support for my mother to get a job she loved." He smiled slightly. "We didn't have much. But we had more than we'd ever had. Until someone serving on the board embezzled funds and the charity shut its doors."

Someone gasped as a quiet murmur swept through the room. Eviana kept her gaze trained on Shaw, strove for calm and collected even as her heart swelled in her chest.

"My mother and I returned to Edinburgh. I missed school half the time to help pay the bills. My mother was only forty-four years old when she passed away from a heart attack after working two shifts back-to-back as a maid and a waitress." His voice roughened, but he didn't falter. "Tonight I'm speaking to you as someone who knew a better life because of the generosity of others. Even though it was taken away, it motivated me to try harder, do better. As I've talked with each of you this evening, I've outlined our plan for doing our best to ensure this doesn't happen again. But I also hope that sharing my motivation to begin the Harrington Foundation will demonstrate my personal commitment and serve as the first step toward earning your trust back."

The quiet was broken by the sound of a soft clap. Eviana looked over to see Olivia Mahs slowly rising to her feet. Others joined in until the whole room was filled with the sounds of applause.

You did it, Shaw.

He had done it. She and Kirstin had helped, given him the tools and resources he'd needed. But he'd been the one to take that final leap, to listen to her advice and bare his soul to the people who had deserted him in one of his darkest hours.

Shaw stood motionless for a few seconds before nodding his head and taking his seat. When he looked toward Eviana's table, she managed to mouth *Well done* as she fought to maintain her composure. As people approached him, she excused herself and stepped out into the gardens.

The garden welcomed her, the floral scents made more potent by the settling of night. She breathed them in as she tried to calm her racing heart, tried to ground herself as she fully accepted in that moment that she was in love with Shaw Harrington. A truth she had denied, one that seemed almost impossible given they'd known each other for less than a month.

But it was there, beautiful and bright and heartbreaking. His confession to a room full of strangers, his commitment to doing the right thing and ensuring others didn't suffer needlessly, had cemented the emotions she had been powerless to stop since the moment he'd first spoken to her on the sidewalk.

"Going well?"

Eviana froze, then slowly relaxed as the voice registered. Jodi sat in a chair off to the side, partially eclipsed by shadows from the lanterns.

"It is." She gave her bodyguard a slight smile. "Very well."

"Good." Jodi paused. "It's not my business, but are you and Mr. Harrington..."

Eviana's cheeks flamed. "We're not lovers, if that's what you're asking."

Jodi held up her hands. "I just don't want you to get hurt."

Too late. Just the thought of leaving him hurts.

"I appreciate it, but—"

"Ana?" Eviana whipped around. Shaw stood just behind her, concern wrinkling his brow. "Who are you talking to?"

Her heart slammed into her throat. "I...no one."

He looked over his shoulder. His eyes narrowed.

"You. You were at the Dome." A frown darkened his face. "I've seen you outside my office, too." His gaze shifted to Eviana. "But only when you've been there."

Jodi stood and moved to Eviana's side. "I'm a friend."

"A friend? Or a stalker?"

Alarm flared in Eviana's belly. "Shaw, it's not what you think—"

"Is that why you've been so secretive? Why you won't talk about home?"

O Bože, what had she done? Why hadn't she told him sooner?

"No, that's not it."

"Then what?" Shaw stepped closer, his gaze still fixed on Jodi's face, shoulders thrown back.

"She's my bodyguard."

It took a moment for the word to register. But then, slowly, Shaw turned to look at her. "Bodyguard?"

"Yes."

He stared at her. "Who are you?"

She nearly broke then. Nearly gave in to the urge to cry. But she squared her shoulders and prepared to face the consequences of her choices.

"Princess Eviana Adamovič of Kelna."

CHAPTER NINETEEN

Shaw

SHAW SLOWLY TURNED his head to look at Ana.

No, Eviana. Princess Eviana.

He glanced back at the blonde woman standing off to the side. Her gaze was fixed on Eviana, her face blank. No, not entirely true. There was a trace of concern in her eyes.

"Princess?"

"Go, Jodi." The words were uttered so softly Shaw barely heard them over the noise of conversation and music from the restaurant behind them. "Please."

Jodi cast him a warning look as she headed inside. He returned it with one of his own. She'd known about Eviana's deception, had let a princess run around the United Kingdom with almost no supervision.

He thought very little of Eviana's bodyguard.

The door clicked shut behind her. Eviana moved away from the windows and wrapped her arms around herself, much as she had that night on the London Eye.

"How does a princess from the Adriatic coast end up in Scotland?"

She flinched at the ice in his voice. "I… I saw a picture of Edinburgh Castle. It reminded me of…" Pink appeared in her cheeks. "The palace back home."

The palace. Eviana lived in an actual palace. His hands curled into fists at his sides as her treachery hit him with full force. Before he could give into it, he gestured for her to follow him. He stalked through the garden, not bothering to look behind him and see if she followed him to a darker corner far from the windows of the dining room. Each step grew heavier in tandem with his rising anger.

Once he was certain they were out of hearing distance, he whirled around and pinned her with his furious stare. "Was it all an act?"

Her brows drew together. "What?"

"Drop the pretense of innocence, An—*Your Highness*. The castle, the Savoy, the train ride… you acted so impressed, so excited—"

"Because I was," Eviana insisted. "I've never stayed at the Savoy, I've never been on a train and the castle—"

"You live in one, Princess." He bit out her title, his tone vicious. But he didn't care. Couldn't care. Not when the world he'd started to embrace over the past month was based on a lie. When the woman he had fallen for didn't exist. "I'm guessing you've flown on private planes and stayed in some of the most exclusive hotels in the world, too."

She looked away. "Everything I said…it was all true."

"Obviously not all of it. You knew how much honesty meant to me."

Her eyes glimmered with unshed tears. "I do. And I wasn't trying to—"

"But you did." He turned away from her, unable to see her face. A face he thought he knew. "Was the thing about your first time in a bar true? Your brother, your sister-in-law?"

"Yes." She sounded broken. Defeated. "My brother is Nicholai Adamoviç, King of Kelna. He and Madeline will marry in October, which is when she'll be crowned queen."

King. Queen. Princess. He'd paid for their tickets on the Eye, the taxi. She'd acted like it had meant something to her.

Just another lie.

"Did you at any point stop to think what ramifications your choices to play commoner could have?"

"What are you talking about?"

He steeled himself, then turned slowly to face her again. She stood in the shadows, her face hollow as she stared at the cobblestones.

"The Harrington Foundation has been in the spotlight for investment fraud." He stepped toward her. "How do you think it would look if it comes out not only that I hired a princess living in disguise to help with my public relations, but that I nearly had an affair with her, too?"

Her head snapped up. "But we didn't—"

"It doesn't matter what we did or didn't do." His voice whipped out as he latched onto his anger, chose it over the anguish trying to fight through and pull him down, pull him back toward her. "What matters is what people think. You know this. You're the one who's been telling me for weeks to be myself, to share a part of myself with others so that they'll trust me when all this time you've been lying to my face."

He'd gone to her that last night on the train, needing to see her, hold her one last time. That memory of her in his arms, the taste of her, the feel of her, had sustained him through the past two weeks. Had been a lifeline tonight as he'd bared his soul.

A memory that now seemed more like a nightmare as he stared down into the face of the woman he had come to care for.

A woman he didn't even know.

A tear slid down her cheek. "Shaw—"

"Mr. Harrington."

She bit down on her lower lip as another tear escaped. "Please… I wanted to…to have just a little bit of normalcy. And then I overheard Kirstin talking about offering an internship and thought

I could learn something that might help me be a better leader—"

"So you used my scandal for your own personal gain?"

A fire kindled in her eyes as her chin came up. "No. And it's grossly unfair of you to accuse me of that."

"It's true," he shot back.

"I can understand your anger over everything but this. You're twisting this to push me even further away." Her voice softened. "I hurt you, and I—"

"I'm not hurt, Your Highness. I'm simply realizing the way I led my life before I met you was the better choice."

Her eyes widened. "That's not true and you know it."

"What I know to be true is that people like you don't get it."

"Like me?"

"People like you—people who have never struggled, who have never known instability or hunger or poverty—don't think. You don't think about the ramifications of your actions. You don't think beyond your own needs."

Silence fell. Eviana had gone unnaturally still, as if she been frozen to the spot. She didn't blink, didn't even appear to breathe. Then, slowly, as if she were coming out from under a spell, she tilted her head to the side. "People like Zach."

A dull roaring began in his ears. Only too late did he realize he had used almost the exact same words he had used to describe Zach the day he'd shown her his mother's picture.

The betrayal was still there. But he knew, even through the gnarled depths of his anger, that Eviana was not like Zach. To suggest such a thing had been more than a step too far. It had been a giant leap off a cliff.

"I didn't mean—"

She held up a hand, the movement smooth and regal. He realized now that all those times he had seen that serene calmness, he had been seeing Princess Eviana Adamovič.

"I did lie," she said. "I lied about my name, and my vagueness and omissions were lies of their own. No, I did not think through the potential ramifications my actions could have on you and the foundation. For that, I am profoundly sorry."

He knew the words were true. But the lack of emotion in her voice, the emptiness in her eyes, clawed at him.

"The one thing I will not let you accuse me of is using your foundation for my own means." Her eyes hardened to emerald chips of ice. There was no fire, no passion. Only a cool detachment. "I meant to tell you tonight if things went well with the dinner, or tomorrow if they didn't. Tell you everything and ask if I could spend my last couple days in Edinburgh with you."

He remembered vaguely now, at the beginning of the party that felt like a lifetime ago. He wanted to say yes, to pretend like the revelations of the last few minutes hadn't just happened.

But even if he had gone too far in comparing her to Zach, it didn't erase that she had lied to him. A crime that so many committed on a daily basis. Yet one that hurt far worse coming from her, after everything he had shared with her.

She stepped away.

"Where are you going?"

"The party is almost over. I'm going home."

Alarm trickled in. "There's still work to be done."

"And Kirstin will do an excellent job for you."

His heart slammed into his ribs as she started to walk toward the covered archway that led back out onto the street.

She stopped walking but didn't turn around. That she wouldn't look at him added another layer of pain to the already heavy weight pressing down on his chest.

"I had hoped you might understand."

"Understand what?" he snapped. How could she expect him to understand her duplicity, her manipulations and clever phrases designed to conceal the truth even as she prompted him to open up?

She looked back at him then, eyes luminous in the glow from a nearby lantern.

"As a princess, there are thousands of people who depend upon me. Stepping into a larger role, that responsibility has grown tenfold." Her fingers tightened into fists, her knuckles turning white. "A princess who's been on the fringes of royal life all of her life because she was the second born. Someone who does what she can and does it well, but also accepted there was little expectation for her to have any large impact. And then her father..."

Her voice caught. He nearly went to her then, as he had in London. But then she was calm once more.

"Her father becomes ill. Her country expands much more rapidly than anyone anticipates. Her brother is left smothered under the weight of everything there is to do." A ghost of a smile played about her lips. "And then he falls in love, and his sister sees an opportunity to stand up, to do the right thing and be a leader."

He stared at her determined not to be pulled in, not to listen to her excuses.

"She does all right. She wasn't born with the expectation of taking on such duties. Even though her father and brother loved her very much, she spent more time with palace staff who constantly corrected her until she didn't really know herself at all."

Shock penetrated his anger. Even in the hardest times, he'd always had his mother's unconditional love.

"But she knows duty." Eviana's voice was barely a whisper now. "And she loves her brother. When duty calls, she handles her new duties. Until she doesn't. Until she starts making little mistakes. She struggles to sleep, struggles to figure out who she's supposed to be. She stumbles during a speech. She's drowning."

Her voice faltered. The images in his mind, of Eviana surrounded by people, struggling to smile, to talk, to do what she had committed to even as she spiraled, redirected his anger to the people who had placed so many demands on her even as they encouraged her to stifle the strengths that made her an incredible woman.

"Her brother recommends she take a sabbatical. One where she can rest and grieve. So she picks a place, one that reminds her of home, but it's still somewhere new. Somewhere she can be normal for just a few months." Her face softened. "She overhears a woman in a coffee shop talking about the kind of person she needs to help grow her business. And the princess thinks not only is this another way to experience life as almost everyone else in the world knows it, but maybe she can learn something. When she goes back home, the small lessons will end up forming the foundation of who she is expected to be."

Eviana smiled then. A perfect smile, one that didn't make her nose slightly wrinkle or her eyes dance. A royal smile.

"I guess I'll find out."

He almost said something, asked her to wait to talk. Pain and pride rendered him silent as she turned and disappeared through the arch into the night.

CHAPTER TWENTY

Eviana
Three months later

THE MORNING SUN bathed the waves of the Adriatic with a rosy glow as Eviana sat on her balcony with a steaming cup of tea. A lark flew by, gifting her with the soft trill of a song as it continued on. A cool October wind brought her the salty scent of the sea.

Home.

She'd started off most mornings like this since she'd returned from Scotland, giving herself half an hour to sit, read or simply enjoy the silence before the palace awoke. On days when her schedule seemed endless, she gave herself an additional fifteen minutes to soak in her tub. It always reminded her of the train ride to London. Most of the time she managed to focus on the nostalgia, reminiscing about the happy moments she had enjoyed on her sabbatical.

But then there were other days where happiness was far out of reach. Days like today when she was sad. Regretful that she had held on to her secrets for so long even as Shaw had slowly opened up. Wondering where he was and what he was doing.

She glanced at her phone, then tightened her fingers around the warm mug. She had made it six weeks and five days before she'd succumbed and looked up the Harrington Foundation online. The one and only article she'd read had been positive, touting the organization's comeback and Shaw's remarkable transformation into the face of the Harrington Foundation. Over ninety percent of the donors had resumed their contributions. The resulting press had led to a surge in donations from the general public in the UK and the States. A fact the newly formed public relations department, mentored by Kirstin Murray of Murray PR, had proudly highlighted. The foundation anticipated being back up to full strength by the end of the year.

Seeing the end result of a project she'd worked on had been gratifying and another boost to her confidence as she'd navigated her return to royal duties. But seeing Shaw's picture, that slight smile that had once made butterflies flap in her chest, had left her near tears. She'd dreamed of him that night, of standing in a capsule as the London Eye rotated. At first it had been wonderful, the dream so real she could feel his touch.

But then the dream had shifted, the Ferris wheel rotating faster and faster as Shaw had backed away from her, his face darkening with pain and anger. He'd looked at her, asking over and over again *Who are you?* as the wheel had spun so fast she could no longer see, no longer tell which way was up or down as the world spun out of control.

She'd woken up in a cold sweat, her heart hammering in her chest as she'd gasped for breath.

She hadn't looked up the foundation or Shaw again. There was no point in torturing herself further. The foundation was moving forward. The goal she had helped work toward had been accomplished. And now she was home. That should have been the end of it.

Except three months later, she still found herself thinking of him. Missing him and what could have been.

The wind blew harder, making the skin of her arms prickle as coldness seeped into her veins at the memory of that night. She had walked through the small stone breezeway to the front of the Witchery and asked Kirstin to meet her outside. Saying she'd felt nauseous hadn't been a lie, but it had certainly been misdirection from the real problem. Thankfully Kirstin had simply told her to go home and rest. The walk back to the apartment had steadied her enough so that she could focus on what had needed to be done to get her out of Scotland as quickly as possible.

Her bodyguard had followed, had started to apologize, but Eviana had stopped her. Jodi had just been doing her job. If she had been honest with Shaw, had not let fear keep her from telling him the truth, none of this would have happened.

Jodi had helped her pack in record time, gone to the store for a box of hair dye and helped her achieve a brown close enough to her normal color until her real color grew back in.

She'd agreed to Jodi's recommendation of booking a private plane instead of flying commercial into Dubrovnik. Jodi had also suggested stopping off somewhere else along the way and using the last few days of Eviana's sabbatical to rest, recuperate. Somewhere like Paris or Lisbon or Zurich. But it'd been as if a switch had been flipped. All Eviana had wanted was to get home.

When she'd arrived, Nicholai and Madeline had surprised her at Kelna's tiny airport. Photographers had caught pictures of them hugging on the tarmac. They'd been splashed across Kelnan and Croatian newspapers the next day, and even a few American outlets, with the headline "The Princess is Home!"

There had been some speculation about where she had spent her nearly three months. She'd waited nearly a week for the axe to fall, for Shaw to reveal what she had been up to as punishment for her deception, or some zealous tabloid journalist unveiling all the sordid details.

But there had been nothing. Just silence.

She filled up her days despite Madeline and

Nicholai's words of caution. No longer did she sit on the fringes, questioning every word that was about to come out of her mouth or if she wasn't portraying the right face for the occasion. She still exhibited diplomacy and compassion. But she had finally found her voice. And she used it.

She'd walked into the Witchery thinking she had conquered so many of her fears. Yet it had been surviving the rejection of the man she had fallen in love with that had given her the final push into completely embracing the woman she had discovered in Edinburgh. To truly embrace the leader she was capable of being.

Not that she was perfect. She'd still made her fair share of mistakes in the past three months. But unlike before, instead of analyzing each and every single one and worrying about it, she'd examined it, taken whatever lesson she could and moved on. No more lingering over old mistakes. No more focusing more on what people thought of her instead of what she could achieve with action.

Madeline and Nicholai had both noticed. So had Helena, even going so far as to compliment the speech Eviana had written herself to announce that the hospital would be adding a new neonatal wing the following year.

There were good things. So many good things. But on days like today, when she closed her eyes and could hear the long whistle of a train, smell spice and wood on the air, feel strong hands cradling her face as if she were made of glass…

On days like today, the good things were hard to find.

A knock sounded on her door. Eviana glanced at her watch and frowned. It was just before seven in the morning. She didn't have any events scheduled until after breakfast.

"Come in," she called over her shoulder.

"Dobro jutro, sestro."

She smiled as Nicholai's voice sounded behind her. He walked out onto the balcony a moment later, dressed in trousers and a navy blue dress shirt.

"It's a quarter 'til seven."

Nicholai arched a brow as he sat down in the lounge chair next to hers. "And?"

She gestured to her bathrobe and fuzzy slippers. "You're making me look bad."

Nicholai chuckled. Despite the challenges of the past year—the losses, the country's explosive growth, the frenzy of media—she couldn't remember the last time Nicholai had looked so happy.

What would it be like to have the kind of relationship he had with Madeline? To have someone love you completely, the good and the bad, to find a compromise like the one he and Madeline had so that they could be together?

Her throat constricted. Even if Shaw had been

able to forgive her, the life she led would have killed him. Her duty was first and foremost to her country, followed by her allegiance to her king and queen. She would not shirk it.

Not even if Shaw had returned her feelings.

Sadness tugged at her. She finally had her confirmation that she was committed to her role. She could mourn what that commitment meant and lean into the love and support of her brother and Madeline instead of keeping her regrets to herself like dirty secrets. She hadn't shared much of what had happened in Edinburgh. But they'd sensed her sadness and supported her.

She snuggled deeper into her chair and watched as the sun climbed higher.

"I think you have a better view than I do," Nicholai said as they watched another lark dip and swirl overhead.

Eviana smirked at him. "It's what I deserve for being second best around here."

She'd meant the words as a joke. But Nicholai frowned at her.

"Is that really how you felt?"

She started to brush off his question to make an excuse or a joke. But then she stopped. Honesty. Authenticity. There would be times when she would not be able to adhere to those concepts. Would have to abstain or dance around the truth. Such was the life of a royal.

But she had vowed when she had returned to be as truthful as she could.

"Yes."

Regret crossed Nicholai's face. "Did I make you feel like that?"

"No. I always felt loved by you and *Otac*. You two just spent so much more time together since you were the heir." She wrinkled her nose. "And the people I spent time with were more old-fashioned. Sit and look pretty, don't speak your mind, etcetera."

"You said last year that you didn't think I trusted you."

She nodded. "It felt like anytime I offered to help, unless it was with a charity, you didn't want my help. Our father was the same way until the last few years. Tradition has always dictated that the second born, and anyone after that, be focused on enriching the lives of Kelnans through charitable works. I accepted that, even if I didn't always understand it. I tried not to let it hurt me." She shrugged. "But sometimes it did. Other times I wondered if it was because I simply wasn't capable and I was overestimating my abilities."

"As Madeleine has reminded me countless times, the old ways are not always the right ones."

Eviana grinned. "I watch that video of her first press conference about once a week."

Nicholai rolled his eyes, but a smile lingered

about his lips. "I almost had a heart attack in the moment."

"It was good for you."

"It was," Nicholai agreed, surprising her with his answer. "I got so used to doing everything on my own and, as you said, thinking about the way things had always been that I never stopped to think about how they could be." He looked at her then, his eyes sad. "I failed you. Not just before Madeline, but after."

Confused, Eviana set her tea on the table and turned to face her brother. "What are you talking about?"

"Before, all I could think about was tradition. Expectations. Everything that Helena drums into our heads. And then after..." His voice trailed off. A muscle worked in his throat as he swallowed hard. "After *Otac* passed, you being there to take on so many of the duties was a lifeline. One I abused."

She reached over and grab her brother's hand. "I told you that I wanted to do this. That I wanted to be more for our country."

Nicholai laid his other hand on top of hers. "I should have told you this months ago, but when you started taking on more, you were...phenomenal."

Tears pricked her eyes. She tried to blink them back. "I... I thought I..."

"No, *sestro.* You're incredible at speaking with people and forming connections. You jumped in

and tackled everything that was thrown at you."
A fond smile lit his face. "You and Madeline are
so much alike in that regard."

Eviana grinned through her tears. "I'll take that
as a compliment."

"You should," Nicholai said earnestly. "I laid
so much at your feet in those months after *Otac*
passed. I was so focused on the shipping port and
the ballroom and the infrastructure assessment
after the bridge collapse that I didn't stop to look
at what it was doing to you."

"I thought…"

"I know. I should have said so much more."

Eviana blinked the rest of her tears away. "I know
you told me I was doing well. But my own insecurities made me think you were just trying to be
nice. And then I started making those mistakes—"

"Everyone makes mistakes."

She hesitated. "I overheard someone say after
I ruined the chamber luncheon speech that you
would never have made that mistake."

Nicholai's eyes hardened. "Who?"

"No."

"Eviana—"

"No, Nicholai. It hurt, but that person was en-
titled to their opinion."

"It was Helena." She froze. Nicholai grinned.
"You still have a terrible poker face."

"Look, Helena and I don't see eye to eye…well,
ever, but—"

"Helena and I had a long discussion while you were gone. Her practices, while admirable in their dedication to the crown, were rooted in how things used to be done. Even she acknowledged that you did well given how quickly you were thrust into it all. Especially right after losing our father."

A disbelieving laugh escaped her. "You're joking."

"I'm not. She was hard on you because she wanted you to succeed. But," he said firmly, "that's not the way things are going to be moving forward."

Eviana shook her head. "I just can't believe… Helena, of all people, giving a compliment."

"You were incredible then, and you're doing even more now. Have you seen everything you've accomplished since you've been back?" he asked when she started to shake her head. "The new wing for the hospital, representing the palace in I don't know how many meetings with ambassadors and dignitaries. Proposing the addition of a railway system to Parliament." He grasped her face between his hands and kissed her forehead. "You are more than capable, Eviana. You're a partner, an equal. It's not just Madeline and I who are fortunate to have you. It's our people."

"Even when I speak my mind?"

"You do so with grace. And you have good ideas. Great ideas. I wonder where you've been hiding them all this time."

She glanced away. She'd had plenty of time to think at night when she lay in bed, waiting for sleep to finally find her. Time to unpack years of memories and habits that had led her to those final days before she'd gone to Scotland.

"Do you remember when I was four and *Otac* was going to England for some conference?"

Nicholai frowned. "I think so, but I don't remember much about it."

"Do you remember me throwing a tantrum and attaching myself to his leg as he tried to walk out of the Grand Hall?"

Nicholai pressed his lips together in an attempt not to smile. "I do."

She sucked in a deep breath. "I remember after he left someone telling me to behave. To be like a princess. It was such a small thing, and it wasn't said meanly. But it stuck with me. Over the years whenever people would remind me to do this or say that instead of what I wanted to, it made me feel like the person I was inside was not…right. That I wasn't capable of being the princess I was supposed to be."

Nicholai's eyes glinted. "How did I not see any of this?"

"Because I didn't let you." Her voice trembled. "Because I wanted to make you and our father proud."

Nicholai looked away and stared out over the sea. "I wish I could say that I have never wanted you to be anyone but who you truly are. But the man I was before I met Madeline versus the man I am today...they're two very different people. I don't know how I would have reacted then if you had jumped in like you are now." He looked back at her, his eyes full of grief. "And for that I'm sorry."

"What matters is now." And she meant it. "Knowing that you approve of what I've been doing, before I left and now, means everything to me."

"I mean every word, Eviana. I don't know what happened on your sabbatical, but when you came back, it was as if you'd..." His voice trailed off as a reluctant smile tugged at his lips. "Madeline said it was as if you'd finally broken free. That you were letting everyone see the real you."

Warmth filled her chest. "She really is amazing."

"She is." Nicholai sobered. "But I still feel like there's something you're not telling me. You seem more yourself. But every now and then, you look...heartbroken."

Because I am. Because I fell in love and didn't trust myself enough to tell him everything when I had the chance.

"My time away had so many positives," she finally said. "Living on my own. Making a friend."

She thought of Kirstin, who had responded to the hastily written resignation letter Eviana had fired off the morning after the dinner party by calling her and demanding to know what was going on. Eviana had answered, more out of obligation than actual desire to talk to her mentor and friend. But it had been one of the best things to happen to her. When she'd told Kirstin the truth, the older woman had stayed silent for what felt like an eternity before finally blurting out, *So do I get to visit you at your palace?*

Mentoring the Harrington Foundation's new public relations department had taken up far too much time to allow for a visit. Until next week. Kirstin would officially be a guest of the royal family at Nicholai and Madeline's wedding.

"I'm glad I didn't know just how much living on your own you were going to be doing until you got back," Nicholai grumbled.

"I know. That's why I didn't tell you," Eviana teased.

"And what about the not so positives? Come on, Evie," he said when she started to look away again. "I can tell something's wrong."

"Not wrong. It's been resolved. It's just... I made some really good friends. People I cared about. And I hurt them." Blue eyes rose in her mind. Warm with affection and longing. Then ice-cold with fury. Hurt. "One in particular."

"You are allowed to make mistakes."

"I know."

She thought back to the numerous times Shaw

had expressed how much honesty meant to him. How much Zach's actions had hurt him. How many times he had told her he liked her for who she was. He'd made her feel like he was the first person to see all of her and like what he saw.

Yet there had been that insidious sliver of doubt that had been buried so deep inside her she hadn't been able to let go and fully let Shaw in. She'd made excuses, some of which had been valid at first when she'd barely known him. But as they'd grown closer, as he'd shared more of himself, she had done what she had accused him of and held back out of fear.

For that, she'd lost him.

"I hope whoever it is realizes how big of a mistake they made in letting you go."

Eviana shook her head even as she smiled. "I appreciate the sentiment. But I haven't talked to them since I came home."

A vice gripped her heart, squeezed tight for one painful second, then released.

One day at a time.

"I doubt I ever will again."

CHAPTER TWENTY-ONE

Shaw

THE SUN SANK behind Edinburgh Castle, giving the timeworn walls a glowing orange outline as day turned to night. Shaw stared at it, his chin braced in one hand.

Three months. It had been three months since Eviana had walked out of the restaurant and out of his life. Three months since he'd talked to her, heard her laugh, seen her smile. Yet every time he turned around, there was something to remind him of her.

Including an ancient castle right outside his window.

Frustrated, he turned away from the window and refocused his attention on his computer. The past twelve weeks had ushered numerous changes into his life. The dinner for the foundation's most prolific donors had exceeded his expectations. Olivia had made a public statement about her decision to renew her contributions, a statement that had been followed by a flood of donations.

Two months later, Zach had been convicted of embezzling funds due to investing far more than he had been approved for by the board. But the ruling had come with a lenient sentencing given all the evidence had pointed to Zach genuinely trying to improve the foundation's financial security.

Shaw had attended the sentencing. When Zach had seen him, he'd gone pale but faced him, regret etched into his face. It had been in that moment that Shaw had accepted that Zach was going to face his punishment. Holding on to his anger did nothing but let a damaging emotion fester.

The picture of him shaking Zach's hand had gone viral, with headlines like "Founder of Charity Forgives Disgraced CEO." The resulting publicity and subsequent surge in donations had left the foundation with triple the amount of money Zach had lost.

The board of trustees had asked Shaw to consider taking the position permanently. He'd declined for the long term but agreed to serve until they found someone to replace Zach. He'd even taken leave from his firm in New York to focus on the foundation and see it through the upcoming transitions. Transitions like the addition of a new public relations department, one currently being mentored by Kirstin Murray.

His eyes darted to the side and fixed on the

castle once more. He had everything he had ever dreamed of.

His life had never seemed emptier.

For the first few weeks after Eviana's departure, he'd managed to hang on to his anger, his wounded pride. But as the days had passed, morbid curiosity had sunk its talons into him until he'd finally caved and looked her up online. Oddly enough, he hadn't doubted her story. He'd simply been too hurt and angry to hear what she'd been saying.

When he'd scroll through the stories dating back to the weeks just before she'd come to Scotland—from her father's funeral to speculations about her weight, if she was sleeping well or feeling replaced by her brother's impending marriage—he'd gained a deeper understanding of the scrutiny she had faced. Everything she said, ate and did was analyzed and picked apart by the international press. He'd gripped the edge of his desk so hard he'd nearly snapped off a piece when he'd read one from just a few weeks ago speculating about Eviana's love life or seemingly lack thereof. The thought of another man holding her hand, getting to see her true smile, had him seeing red.

But there had also been the stories that had reinforced the image of the Eviana he'd known. The one that had lodged itself in his mind was a story of a bridge collapse the year prior. Many of the stories had focused on Eviana's future sister-in-law, mostly because a nurse had snapped a photo of the queen-to-be holding a child who had been injured in the collapse. But there had been other stories, too, ones that had highlighted Eviana's years of dedication and hard work to the hospital, including helping arrange fundraising events, galas and visiting numerous patients every week.

The photos of her with children in the hospital had hit him especially hard. His heart had twisted in at the sight of Eviana's beautiful face so happy as she'd sat and drawn silly pictures with a toddler. It had been those photos, the ones of her with the organization she had poured her soul into, that showed the Eviana he'd known. Happy, optimistic, content.

The others, however… The other photos had made him want to lash out. Photos of her dressed in pastel colors, her face blank as she attended dozens of events to merely serve as window dressing. He had been exhausted by his brief time under the microscope of the international press. Eviana had lived her whole life under one. Not just lived it, but questioned it, doubted it, even if she persevered and had tried to be the kind of leader she thought her country deserved.

Although, he remembered, the more recent pictures had been different. No more pastels or bland expressions. She'd been snapped in a bright red dress at a museum opening and a lavender skirt while out shopping with her sister-in-law. She hadn't looked vibrantly happy. But she'd seemed more confident. More herself.

A sight that had made him simultaneously proud and ache that he wasn't there to experience her renaissance.

Shaw scrubbed a hand over his face as he slammed his laptop shut. The more time passed, the more her absence pressed on him. He missed her sunny smile, listening to her ideas, sitting and working in the same space and simply enjoying her presence. She had woven herself into his life so deeply it was impossible to get rid of her.

And he didn't want to. He had been so focused on his own pain and pride the night of the dinner at the Witchery that he hadn't stopped to think. To listen.

As he stared out over Edinburgh, he finally acknowledged that this had been his problem for years. His obsession with doing better than the people who had let him and his mother down, of hanging on to betrayal and grief. It had blinded him to the world around him. His experience with the charity in London and the transgressions that had cost him and his mother so much had left him with exceedingly high standards. Important ones, but ones so high almost no one could reach them.

Something he had done out of fear. When everyone fell short and he had a reason to keep them at arm's length, no one could get close enough to hurt him.

Until now. Until Eviana had slipped in with her sunny smile and kindness tempered by that confidence that would carry her far if she would just trust herself.

As he should have trusted her.

The vise around his chest tightened. Slowly, he opened his laptop back up and pulled up the news site he'd been frequenting. An American reporter was in Kelna covering the week leading up to the wedding. The most recent article included photos of Eviana with the bride-to-be enjoying coffee at a local café. The bodyguard he'd identified, Jodi, sat at another table in the background, along with another man he assumed to be an additional bodyguard. The future queen, Madeline, had been showing Eviana something on her phone. Eviana had worn sunglasses, so he hadn't been able to see her eyes. The photographer had caught her mid-smile. But even with the sunglasses, he could tell it wasn't her usual smile. The one that made her eyes crinkle at the corners.

Was royal life weighing on her once more? Or did his rejection still linger, hurting her over and over again despite the months of no contact?

He reached out, traced a finger over her face framed by her dark hair. It had been a jolt the first time he'd looked her up and seen her with dark brown hair. Yet it had seemed more…her.

God, he missed her.

Shaw clicked out of the screen. Where would

he even begin in mending the broken fences between them? Was there a point? Her life was, and always would be, in Kelna. His was…

He stopped. He had his house here in Edinburgh. A pleasant space, but nothing special. This building, his office—they were all simply there, tools to be used to further the mission of the Harrington Foundation. He'd barely used the office in the past three years as Zach had taken over so much of the duties. He had a small fortune earning interest every day.

None of it made him happy. The only thing in his current life that brought him pleasure was the foundation. When the new CEO took over, he wanted to stay involved, attend at least some of the events the new public relations team was coming up with. Wanted to visit the charities and people the foundation benefited, see firsthand what was going well and what could be done better.

But to let the Harrington Foundation truly grow, he would have to let it go. To trust others with more expertise and skill to nurture it.

Which left him with…nothing. Nothing except a small manor house in Greenhill and a luxurious penthouse in New York City he hadn't thought of even once since he'd come back to Edinburgh.

What he had thought of, the one person who had never left his thoughts, even when his anger had been all-consuming, had been Eviana. She had brought out the best in him. And he missed her. He wanted her in his life. Wanted…

His heart slammed into his ribs. He wanted it all. A life with Eviana and all that entailed. Living in Kelna, marriage… Even though the thought of having children terrified him, it wasn't hard to imagine Eviana with their baby in her arms. Exploring a castle with a dark-haired toddler or riding a train to visit a new country with a redheaded child bouncing on the seat next to him.

It wouldn't be all sunshine. There would be hard times, too. Just the thought of having photographers constantly swarm around made him scowl.

But he'd stepped outside of his comfort zone numerous times over the past few months. Each time had gotten a little easier. Putting himself out there for the sake of the foundation had made it more manageable. If the price to pay for being with Eviana was to be in the spotlight, he would gladly pay it over and over.

"I love her."

Shaw said the words softly at first, then repeated them again. He was in love with a princess.

He turned back to his computer and pulled up flights to Kelna. That was how Kirstin found him when she walked in three minutes later, on the phone with his secretary and running an irritated hand through his hair. He shot her a glance and gestured for her to take a seat.

"All flights are booked?" he asked irritably.

"Yes, sir," his secretary said slowly, as if she hadn't just told him that exact same thing. "I've checked every airline. There are no flights into Dubrovnik. People are flying into Croatia so they can travel into Kelna for the royal wedding."

He blew out a frustrated breath. "Fine. Look for anything into nearby airports."

"I'll try, sir, but it might not—"

"Just try." He stopped himself. "Please."

Shaw hung up.

"Where are you off to?" Kirstin asked with an arched brow.

"I'm trying to get to Kelna."

There was a beat of quiet. And then she exploded out of her chair, a huge grin on her face. "I knew it!"

"Knew what?"

"You're in love with Eviana!"

He sat back in his chair as he narrowed his eyes at her. "What makes you think that?"

"Oh, please," Kirstin scoffed as she sat back down. "One, I have eyes. Two, you've been a mopey mess ever since she left."

He scowled. "You said I was nicer."

"You are. But you're still walking around like you have your own personal thundercloud perpetually raining on you."

"Thanks."

"And," she continued as she shot him a smug

smile, "because Eviana's been a sad mess ever since she left, too."

His breath froze in his chest. And then he leaned forward, his attention riveted on Kirstin. "You've spoken to her?"

She crossed one leg over the other. "Those four personal days I've booked? They're to attend the royal wedding as Eviana's guest. She even invited my mother."

His throat constricted. "How...how is she?"

"Well. She's made quite her mark on the palace since she came back."

"I read about everything she's doing." His smile was tinged with pride. "She's presenting a proposal on the addition of a new railroad to the minister and Department of Transportation."

"And continuing her work with the hospital charity, along with several others. We talk once a week. She thought I was going to be angry at her."

"But you weren't?"

"It bothered me for a few seconds. Then I realized it didn't matter if her name was Ana or Her Royal Highness Princess Eviana," Kirstin said with a shrug. "Or if she was a blonde or a brunette. She came through for me during a very difficult time in my life. She created an excellent campaign for you and achieved results. I'm getting new business because of the work she did. And I gained a new friend."

He looked away. If only he had been as understanding and forgiving instead of holding on to the familiar pain and pride that had guided so much of his adult life.

"She's sad," Kirstin said gently.

"I hurt her."

"You did. But I think she knows she hurt you, too."

"She did. It doesn't excuse my reaction, how I just let her walk away. But I'm going to rectify that. If I can…" His voice trailed off as inspiration struck. "How are you getting to Kelna?"

Kirstin leaned back. "Don't even think about it. I'm all for true love, but if you think I'm giving up my ticket when this will be the only chance I have in my life to attend a royal wedding—"

"If I can persuade her to forgive me and hear me out, you might be a bridesmaid in the next one."

Kirstin stared at him for a moment, eyes huge and round. And then she jumped up again, let out a loud whoop and ran around the desk to wrap him in an enthusiastic hug.

"She hasn't said yes yet—"

"If she doesn't, I'll help you come up with a plot to kidnap her or something like they do in the romance books until she admits she's in love with you, too."

He winced. "How about I just start with an apology and telling her I love her?"

"That works, too." Kirstin frowned. "But how

are you going to get there if the flights are sold out?"

"That's why I was asking what your plans were. I've never booked a private jet for myself before, but I would prefer to have company if I'm going to spend the money on it."

Kirstin clapped her hands together. "I swear, this day just keeps getting better and better."

CHAPTER TWENTY-TWO

Eviana

EVIANA WALKED OUT of the small boutique on Lepo Plavi's main thoroughfare, a pale blue gift bag in her hand. Out of the corner of her eye, she spied two photographers with their cameras aimed at her. She smiled at Jodi as they walked down the sidewalk. "At least we're down to two instead of the four that followed us here."

"I can't wait until this wedding's over," Jodi growled.

Her bodyguard's furious expression made her laugh. Something she desperately needed. As much as she was looking forward to the wedding tomorrow, there would also be no shortage of relief once Madeline and Nicholai flew off to their honeymoon in Bora Bora. Hordes of tourists and paparazzi had descended on the capital. While Nicholai and Madeline were certainly the focus, Eviana had also become a target of random people wanting her autograph or to snap a selfie with a real princess.

It hadn't helped that one magazine had obtained a photo of from last month's hospital gala of her standing off to the side and watching people dance. The expression on her face hadn't been sad, but she hadn't looked joyful, either. The headline had read "Will Bachelorette Princess Find Her Own Prince Charming?"

The resulting media attention, not to mention a surge in the number of men asking her out on dates to the museum, local wineries or one of Kelna's many restaurants, had left her wanting to hide in her room.

Logically, she should've been flattered. But she had zero interest in any of the men who had reached out. Not that they weren't interesting and accomplished, from an ambassador she had met last year to a professional football player from Croatia.

Maybe next year.

For now, she simply told everyone that her first and primary focus was supporting her brother and his soon-to-be wife on one of the biggest days of their lives.

She kept the part about having a broken heart to herself.

"Are you sure you wouldn't like me to call for the car?" Jodi asked as one photographer moved into the middle of the sidewalk and snapped a half dozen photos in a matter of seconds.

"As soon as I do that, they win. Besides," she

added with a smirk, "maybe they'll catch a photo I could use on my dating-app profile next year."

Jodi stared at her for a moment before breaking out into a grin. "No disrespect, Your Highness, but I would pay to see your brother's reaction when you tell him you're going on a dating website."

Eviana was about to respond when she caught movement out of the corner of her eye. Awareness crackled across her skin as a man emerged from the Grand Hotel.

It can't be.

But she knew that determined gait, the thick red hair, the angular jaw covered by that closely trimmed beard. His head suddenly jerked to the side, and a deep blue gaze met hers. Fierce emotion flared in his eyes before he blinked and his familiar mask slid back into place.

She wanted nothing more than to turn away, to leave before she said or did something that would reveal her feelings. But she couldn't. Not with so many people milling about, so many photographers with cameras ready to document her every move.

"Your Highness," Jodi murmured, warning in her voice.

"I know." She gritted her teeth even as she smiled. "Just play along."

Shaw stayed where he was on the sidewalk as they approached.

Steady, she told herself. *You can do this.*

"Mr. Harrington."

His eyes narrowed before he bowed his head. "Your Highness."

She didn't burst into tears or fling herself into his arms.

So far, so good.

"I didn't realize you—"

"Your Highness."

Eviana's polite smile froze in place as Joseph Rexford, an ambassador from the States, emerged from the hotel and spotted her.

"Good morning, Ambassador."

"Good morning," he said with a friendly smile as he approached. "I'm looking forward to…" His voice trailed off as he noticed Shaw. "Shaw Harrington?"

Shaw turned his head, then smiled slightly. "Ambassador. It's good to see you again."

The two men shook hands. Even over the passing traffic and rise and fall of conversations around her, Eviana swore she could hear the click of the cameras across the street, down the block.

Smile. Smile.

"Small world," she said as politely as she could manage.

"Yes. Mr. Harrington and I met last month at a fundraiser at the New York Public Library. He was there with…" Joseph snapped his fingers. "Kirstin

Murray. Getting ideas for upcoming events for the Harrington Foundation."

Despite the pain and heartache thumping inside her chest, Eviana smiled.

"The comeback has been impressive." She looked at Shaw. "You have a lot to be proud of."

Did she imagine the look in his eyes, the longing?

"How are you two acquainted?"

Eviana looked back at Joseph, who was now regarding her and Shaw with a slight degree of suspicion.

"Actually, I was introduced to Mr. Harrington by Ms. Murray," Eviana said with a light laugh. "I spent time in Edinburgh during my sabbatical and made both of their acquaintances there."

"I didn't realize that's where you'd been staying."

She lowered her gaze. "My whole trip was very private."

The ambassador's eyes widened. "Of course. I'm sorry."

"No need," Eviana said smoothly. "My brother and Madeline were gracious in giving me time off to rest and recuperate. But Ms. Murray and Mr. Harrington were also very generous to me with their time and sharing their experiences. It gave me a new insight into public relations and professional communications."

"Lessons I noticed you incorporated into your work here in Kelna these last couple of months."

Shaw's words sent a bolt of pleasure through her. Had he been thinking about her as often as she thought about him?

"Thank you."

"It'll be nice to have another familiar face at the wedding," Joseph said with a smile aimed in Shaw's direction.

"I'm not here for the wedding." His hesitation was so slight that Eviana wondered if the ambassador had even noticed it. "My timing is poor, but I'm here because after the wedding, I hope to meet with Her Highness and discuss the possibility of her presence at some of our events next year. Given her interest in supportive causes like mine, having a royal as an official patron would do wonders for the foundation."

Her pleasure evaporated. Blunt anger swiftly replaced it. Was that really the only reason why he was here? To use her?

"An opportunity I'm happy to discuss. Although," she continued as she fought to keep the edge out of her voice, "with the usual drop-off in guests at the last minute, we would be delighted to host you tomorrow for the wedding."

He inclined his head again. She wanted to scream at the formality of their interaction, play-acting for the sake of the cameras. The exact opposite of what their relationship had been.

"I look forward to it," he said. "Thank you."

"Jodi will send a formal invitation over this afternoon." She glanced at her watch. "Speaking of, I have a gift that needs to be delivered to the bride-to-be. Ambassador, Mr. Harrington." She gave them each a formal nod. "We look forward to seeing you tomorrow."

She held it together down the street, not looking back, not faltering in front of the cameras.

Perhaps this was all a test. Putting her in another stressful situation, one where she had to come up with something on the spur of the moment with scores of people watching. No, it hadn't been a speech delivered to influential business leaders in the community. But there had been a different type of audience present, one far more intimidating and even, daresay, dangerous. The kind of people who snapped photos that could easily be taken out of context or twisted to fit a narrative to sell more stories.

"Call the car, please."

She felt Jodi's eyes on her. "I can have him kicked out of the country."

Eviana tried, and failed, not to smile. "As tempting as that offer is, I will have to pass. He'll come to the wedding tomorrow. There will be plenty of people there he can interact with. Especially if his goal is truly to use this event to expand the foundation."

"If it is," Jodi bit out, "I still have contacts in the Navy who I'm sure could—"

"I appreciate you, Jodi."

Out of the corner of her eye, she saw Jodi's look of surprise. "Thank you, Your Highness."

"You gave me a gift back in Edinburgh, one I'm not sure many would have. Being able to live my life the way I wanted to, on my own terms, to feel like I was just an everyday person. I desperately needed it."

"You're welcome." Jodi exhaled. "Although I still feel like I failed you."

"How so?"

"I failed to protect you from him."

Her heart twisted. "You didn't fail. It didn't have the happily-ever-after that I prefer, but I will never regret my time with him."

Even if it felt like her heart was being shattered all over again, leaving bits and pieces trailing behind her as she once more walked away from the man she loved.

"He's a fool," Jodi growled as a black car pulled up to the curb.

"On that," Eviana replied softly as another guard got out and opened the door for her, "we agree."

CHAPTER TWENTY-THREE

Eviana

THE DAY OF the wedding dawned bright and cool. Autumn in Kelna was truly beautiful, with beech and oak trees displaying a dazzling array of colorful leaves in shades of rich red, vibrant orange and cheery yellow. The sky seemed even bluer than in summer, especially when one got up early enough to enjoy the crisp mornings. It was usually one of Eviana's favorite times of year.

But now, as she wandered through the palace gardens on the morning of her brother's wedding, the only emotion she could find was grief. Grief that her father wasn't here to see his only son get married. Grief that their mother had passed far too soon to see either of her children grow into adults.

And grief for the man who probably still slept in a bed just a few kilometers away.

After she had run into him yesterday, Eviana had managed to make it through the rest of the afternoon and evening with a smile on her face. Mostly by sheer will, but she'd done it. She'd laughed and joked through the afternoon at the spa with Madeline, Madeline's mother and some of Madeline's friends from America. She'd conversed with countless people at the dinner following the rehearsal at the chapel.

It hadn't been until she made it into the privacy of her room that she'd succumbed to the need to cry.

He wasn't here to offer forgiveness or his own apology. To ask for just a little more time before they went their separate ways. No, he wanted to use her. Use her name and her legacy.

Her heart clenched. The woman in her wanted to say no to his request, wanted to cut off anything and everything to do with Shaw. She didn't know if she would be able to heal, to move on with her life with him always on the fringes. But the princess in her, the one who understood sacrifice and duty, knew how many people she could help by putting aside her personal feelings and agreeing to his request.

Wasn't that one of the reasons she had fallen in love with Shaw? His commitment to doing the right thing and, as she had later learned, striving to be better than the man who had let down him and his mother, along with countless others? A man who had taken a horrific experience and turned it into something good.

Although in this context, she thought glumly,

his commitment was a double-edged sword. One that cut her deep.

Maybe after the holidays, she could take a short break. A week away, somewhere far flung where she could have another taste of being able to walk down the street and not be recognized...

Footsteps sounded behind her. Irritation cut through her melancholy mood. There were a number of people staying at the palace, including Kirstin and her mother. Mostly close friends and family, along with a few high-profile guests. It was only natural that somebody else would want to enjoy the pleasures of the gardens in the fall.

I just wish they could do it somewhere else.

She turned to greet the intruder. And froze.

Shaw stood just a few feet away, his gaze fixed on her. Hands clenched at his sides. "Good morning."

She swallowed hard. "Good morning, Mr. Harrington."

He took one step forward, as if testing the waters. "It's just us. You don't need to stand on pretense."

"I'm not."

His jaw hardened, an action that drew her eye and nearly made her miss the hurt in his gaze at her curt answer. An answering pain surged in her chest, followed almost immediately by anger. He had no right to be hurt. Not after what he'd said when they had last parted. Not after the reasons he had given yesterday of why he was here, especially the week of her brother's wedding.

"The last time we spoke—"

"Can we not?"

She abandoned all attempts at civility, at maintaining her emotional distance. In this moment, seeing him stand in her place of refuge, so near she could close the distance between them with a couple of steps and touch his face, was too much.

"I understand there are things you want to talk to me about," she said as she lifted her chin, "but they will have to wait until after the wedding."

"That's not—"

"Enjoy the ceremony, Mr. Harrington."

She turned and walked away as fast as her training would allow her to without actually running from him. She blinked back tears, needing the sanctity of her own room. Somewhere she could shut and lock the door against the outside world.

Eviana was crossing the lawn toward her private entrance when Shaw caught up to her, his hand engulfing hers. She hated that her breath caught, that her chest tightened at the contact.

"Don't." She glanced around. She couldn't handle it if a photo of them ended up in the news. The questions she'd have to answer, the renewed scrutiny of her love life. "Not here."

His fingers tightened around hers. "Eviana, please—"

It was the first time he had said her name, her

real name, without pain or fury. It made her pause. Made her want to—

"No. You made your feelings perfectly clear back in Edinburgh." She let herself savor the pressure of his fingers, the warmth of his skin on hers one final time, then yanked her hand out of his. "I can't do this. Not now. I'm going to be standing next to my brother and the future queen of this country in four hours. I don't know why you're here or why—"

"I'm trying to tell you," he growled.

"And I don't want to hear it," she snapped back. "I have spent the last three months trying to move on. Then you show up and bring all of it crashing back. Today of all days I can't be weak, and you, Shaw Harrington, are my weakness."

With that pronouncement, she turned and walked off. It took a moment for her to realize she was walking in the opposite direction she had intended and was heading back toward the rose garden, but she didn't care. She just needed to get away.

The white pebbled circles of the rose maze beckoned to her. She passed under the stone arches, moved past the rose bushes that held on to their blooms thanks to the warmer Mediterranean temperatures. A still-bubbling fountain dominated the center. She slipped past it, her feet carrying her over the familiar stone path that led to a place that she had thought of as hers since childhood.

Even as hurt squeezed her lungs and made her breaths shallow, the white terrace built onto the cliffside eased some of the heartache. How many times had she snuck out here as a child, spinning around the terrace or leaning on the railing to stare at the sea below?

When the photos had come out of Nicholai and Madeline kissing after a royal ball, she had felt horrible for her brother. But the romantic in her had also thought there had been something telling about the location of where they had shared their kiss. The place she had once considered magical.

Now the magic lay in its comfort, its familiarity and offer of refuge.

She moved to the edge and placed her hands on the railing, staring down at the deep blue waves rising and falling against the cliffside. She'd handled that badly—all of her training gone out the window at the mere sight of him. She would've been angry with herself if she weren't so exhausted.

The soft crunch of gravel met her ears. Her body tensed a moment before his voice washed over her.

"Eviana."

It's better this way, she told herself as she stared out over the sea. *Get it out of the way so I can once and for all close this chapter of my life.*

"Say what you came to say and then leave. Please."

Warm hands grasped her shoulders and slowly turned her around. She looked up into his familiar face, into eyes so much like the sea.

"I was wrong."

She stood motionless, the distant roar of the sea indistinguishable from the roar of blood in her ears. "What?"

"I was wrong," he repeated, his voice vibrating with emotion. "I was shocked and hurt, and I let my foolish pride rule that conversation. I never should have let you walk out of that garden"

His hand came up, slowly, then settled on her face. A tremble passed through her as she closed her eyes and leaned into his touch. "Letting you walk away is the biggest regret of my life."

Eviana drew in a shuddering breath, then opened her eyes. She stood at a crossroads. One where she could do as he had done to her and push him away.

Or she could be brave once more. Be brave and give him the honesty she should have so long ago.

"My biggest regret is not trusting you sooner," she said.

"I don't know what it's like to be a royal. To have to guard my identity—"

"But that wasn't all of it." She had to be truthful, had to let him know everything. "In the beginning, yes, I didn't tell anyone because my whole reason for being in Edinburgh was to have a few months where I didn't have to be a princess. Where I could finally breathe. But as I got to know you, I wasn't worried so much about maintaining my anonymity as I was about how you would react when you found out who I was."

"Why?"

Honesty. Truth.

"Because I fell in love with you." His eyes widened, but she rushed on, not wanting to stop. "Because I wasn't confident in who I was. My feelings about the role I'm taking on were so conflicted, and knowing how you feel about being in the spotlight made any possibility of us seem hopeless. And when you said what you did about me being like Zach—"

"Which was a mistake," he cut in, his voice rough. "Something I said in a moment of pain and anger." He held her face in his hands. "You are nothing like him. That I even suggested you were is a guilt I will carry for the rest of my life."

"Still… I am sorry."

"I know. You apologized that night, and I should have accepted your apology. It took a moment to think and process what you told me. Most of all," he said as he rested his forehead against hers, "I should have realized then how much you mean to me. I'm sorry for so many things, including how long it took for me to realize how deeply in love with you I am."

She leaned back, her eyes searching his face. But all she saw was love, love and that deep longing she had glimpsed yesterday on the street but hadn't wanted to believe was possible. "You love me?"

"With all that I am."

He pressed a kiss to her forehead, one that made her heart swell. Then he stepped back. "You said you didn't care why I was here. But I hope I can change your mind."

There, on the terrace where she had dreamed of love and her own Prince Charming, Shaw dropped to one knee and pulled a box out of his pocket. Her hands flew to her lips as he opened it and unveiled a sparkling emerald set in a silver band.

"I never imagined myself falling in love. I never thought about getting married. Having a family. But I'm in love with you. The strong, confident woman who first ensnared me. The calm, elegant royal who guided me through some of the most challenging times I've ever experienced. Most of all, I love your kind heart. That and your ability to take joy in the little things." His blue eyes glinted. "You brought me back to life, Eviana, and I don't want to picture it without you in it."

How was it even possible to fall to the deepest depths of grief, only to be catapulted up into the most incredible moment of happiness she'd ever known?

Except...how could she accept him? Bring him into the life that had been such a struggle for her?

"Shaw..."

"Please tell me that's a yes."

"I want to say yes." Her voice broke. "I love you. You saw me for who I was, believed in me even when I wasn't sure who I was at my core. I want a life with you. But my life is here and—"

"If you accept me, I want to be here for you. I still want to be involved with the foundation," he added as she continued to stare at him, at a loss for words as he offered her everything she'd dreamed of. "But the rest of my life… It's not the same without you, Eviana. Everything I've done up to this point has been for the foundation. It does good work, but I want more. I know that I could do a great deal, not just for you but for your country."

Hope—beautiful, impossible hope—bloomed in her chest. "What are you saying?"

"You told me the reason you fled to Edinburgh was out of exhaustion. Out of fear that you weren't enough. You are enough. You are so much more than you give yourself credit for. But just as your brother faced too much, you do, too. Your brother has Madeline. And I want you to have me. I know absolutely nothing about being married to a royal or what I'd have to do. But if I can survive the finance world of New York, an international investment-fraud scandal and," he added with a slight smile, "dinner with a dozen people who didn't trust me to take care of their money, I know I can be there for you. And what I don't know, I can learn. Want to learn," he added, his voice deepening with emotion, "for you."

His offer, what he was willing to sacrifice hit her like a freight train.

For one horrible moment, she faltered. "What if it's too much?"

"There will be days where it probably will be too much. But we'll have each other. That is worth more to me than any mundane existence could offer." His fingers tightened around hers. "Please say yes, Eviana."

"Yes."

Her answer came out on a whisper. But Shaw heard it, a smile breaking across his face as he pulled the ring out of the box and slid it onto her finger before he stood and pulled her into his arms.

And then he kissed her. A soul-searing kiss that had her seeing stars.

"How is this possible?" she murmured against his lips.

"Kirstin."

She leaned back and laughed. "Kirstin?"

"And Jodi."

"Jodi?" Eviana shook her head slightly. "But she…"

"Oh, she made her feelings clear when she called me last night."

Mortification mixed with amusement. "She called you?"

"Yes. Apparently it's very easy for a former intelligence officer with Kelna's Royal Navy to get information like a personal phone number. She also had some very creative threats on how she planned to remove me from your country. But," he said as grazed his knuckles over her cheek, "when I told her what I had planned and sent her a picture of the ring as evidence of my intentions, she helped me get into the palace this morning."

"Given how well this turned out, I suppose I can't be mad at her. In fact," she said with a small laugh, "I'll probably have to make her a bridesmaid."

His hold on her waist tightened. "How long do we have to wait after your brother's wedding?"

"There's not an official waiting period."

Eviana glanced around the terrace. She could see it now: garlands of roses and ivy wound around the railing. Lanterns flickering as the sun set. The people they loved celebrating their incredible journey.

And Shaw waiting for her at the end of a petal-strewn path, love shining from his eyes as he said *I do*.

"I wouldn't mind a spring wedding," she said.

Shaw lowered his head and captured her mouth with his once more. His low moan reverberated through her, stirring the desire that had nearly consumed them on the train. Her hands slid up his arms, over his shoulders, then up his neck, her fingers tangling in his hair…

The soft chimes of an alarm sounded.

With a regretful sigh, she pulled back to glance down at her watch, then did a double take. "I have to be in my room in five minutes!"

Shaw held up her left hand. "I suppose this will have to come off for the wedding."

"Probably," she said with regret. "I want today to be about Nicholai and Madeline. And given that there have been so many articles about my bachelorette status…"

"No more." Shaw's growl made her toes curl. "As soon as it's allowed, I want the world to know that you're mine."

She smiled up at him. "Now and forever."

EPILOGUE

Shaw
Five years later

A SHARP CRY pierced the stillness of early morning. Shaw sat straight up in bed, his heart thumping. There was an empty space next to him, the sheets in a tangle as if they'd been tossed back in a hurry. "Eviana?"

A moment later his wife appeared in the door, cradling a mound of blankets making soft, blubbering coos. "Just a hungry girl."

His heart swelled as Eviana sat on the bed next to him, her hair mussed as she gazed down at Lucinda Kirstin. At four months old, their daughter had demonstrated her healthy lungs on numerous occasions.

Although, he admitted as he reached over and stroked a finger over the tiny hand that had emerged from the blanket, the recent travel had not helped Lucy's sleeping.

In the five years since he and Eviana had married, they had managed to schedule several weeks off throughout the year where they traveled, mostly in Europe but even to places like Japan and Egypt. Those breaks had helped them both balance the long list of duties they had tackled as Kelna's newest royal couple.

He would never get used to the photographers, to having what he had for lunch at a meeting with an ambassador posted on a gossip website. But seeing the difference his and Eviana's work did, from the charities they supported to advocating for and working toward initiatives like Kelna's soon-to-be-opened railroad that would connect the country with the extensive Eurail system, had been far more rewarding than he had anticipated. Sharing duties with Nicholai and Madeline, who had welcomed him with open arms upon their return from their honeymoon, had made settling into royal life a much easier adjustment than he had anticipated, even allowing for him to stay involved with the continuously growing Harrington Foundation.

Still, he thought as Eviana scooted back and leaned against the headboard, the trip this year was very much needed. With the new addition to their family, they had returned to somewhere familiar. Somewhere they could still enjoy their time away but also savor every moment of new parenthood they could.

He glanced out the window. Mist swirled and

shifted over the green hills as sunlight glimmered on the horizon.

"I think she's trying to compete with the hawk from yesterday," Eviana murmured as Lucy blinked at them, her face serene now that she had both her parents' attention.

It had been Madeline's idea for the royal family to travel to Scotland this summer, a trip that included Nicholai, Madeline, their three-year-old son, Asher, and their eight-month-old daughter, Sarah. They had found a secluded castle in the Highlands for rent, one with acres upon acres of rolling pastures, bubbling creeks and a full-time staff that included a stable caretaker and a hawker.

"Good morning, Lucy," Shaw said.

His daughter's head turned slightly, her eyes widening as they fixed on his face. Emerald eyes, just like her mother, but the little wisps of hair on her head were dark red.

"How about I hold her? Let you get a little more sleep?"

Eviana hesitated for just a moment before she gently laid Lucy in his embrace.

"Just a few more minutes," she said quietly as she lay back down.

"Take all the time you need," he murmured.

A moment later, Eviana's quiet breathing reached his ears. Lucy seemed to understand her mother's need for sleep as she lay quietly in his arms and stared up at him. When he and Eviana had finally decided to start a family of their own, he'd been excited and terrified in equal measure. The same emotions had coursed through him when he'd heard the steady thump of Lucy's heartbeat for the first time, and again when he had seen the little blob on the ultrasound.

But when the nurses had laid his and Eviana's daughter in his arms, it was as if the rest of his world, the last little piece he hadn't even known had been missing had slid into place.

He smiled down at Lucy. "Your grandmothers would have adored you."

Lucy's lips curved up into the tiniest of smiles. His heart stopped as his own smile grew.

"We're not going to tell your mother that your first smile was for me."

His daughter grinned as she let out a soft babble. His arms tightened around her tiny body as he laid a kiss on her forehead. "You are an amazing creature, Lucinda Kirstin Harrington."

Eviana's eyes fluttered. Her gaze slid between him and Lucy, a smile of pure contentment and love on her face. "I love you, Shaw."

"And I love you, Eviana."

Her eyes drifted shut once more. As Shaw sat next to his sleeping wife, with his daughter in his arms and the sun rising over the Highlands, he knew that he had truly found his happily-ever-after.

* * * * *

*If you enjoyed this story,
check out this other great read
from Scarlett Clarke*

The Prince She Kissed in Paris

Available now!

HARLEQUIN
Reader Service

Enjoyed your book?

Try the perfect subscription for Romance readers and get more great books like this delivered right to your door.

See why over 10+ million readers have tried Harlequin Reader Service.

Start with a Free Welcome Collection with free books and a gift—valued over $20.

Choose any series in print or ebook.
See website for details and order today:

TryReaderService.com/subscriptions